A Rifle by the Door

By

Dan Fuller

A RIFLE BY THE DOOR BY DAN FULLER
Published by Trailblazer Western Fiction
an imprint of Lighthouse Publishing of the Carolinas
2333 Barton Oaks Dr., Raleigh, NC 27614

ISBN: 978-1-64526-189-6
Copyright © 2019 by Dan Fuller
Cover design by Elaina Lee
Interior design by Karthick Srinivasan

Available in print from your local bookstore, online, or from the publisher at:
ShopLPC.com

For more information on this book and the author, visit:
https://danlfullercountrywriter.wordpress.com

Brought to you by the creative team at Lighthouse Publishing of the Carolinas (LPCBooks.com): Eddie Jones, Shonda Savage Whitworth, Jennifer Uhlarik, Brian Cross, Jennifer Leo, and Ann Knowles

Library of Congress Cataloging-in-Publication Data
Fuller, Dan.
A Rifle by the Door / Dan Fuller 1st ed.

Printed in the United States of America

Praise for *A Rifle by the Door*

Just finished a read on Dan's new book *A Rifle by the Door* reading it straight through in one sitting. It's an action packed western, fast moving and exciting, but it is even more. It's a coming of age story, told through the eyes of a young boy forced to grow up fast in the midst of the action. It also has a heart-warming faith message that can't help but draw you in. Easily recommended for lovers of a good western tale, but this one will even appeal to the ladies as well.

~**Terry Burns**
Retired agent for Hartline Literary Agency

I couldn't wait for Saturday mornings for "A cloud of dust and a mighty 'Hi Ho, Silver.' The Lone Ranger!" Dan Fuller's novel took me back to "those thrilling days of yesteryear" with his vivid descriptions and "daring and resourceful" characters as they "fight for law and order in the early west." Anyone who loves westerns—and even those who don't—will thoroughly enjoy *A Rifle by the Door*. I'm giving it five silver bullets.

~**James Watkins**
Award-winning author

Dan Fuller's colorful writing style offers the right amount of detail and depth mixed with humor and emotion. This action-packed novel will pull you into its grasp until the very end.

~**Linda Hanna and Deborah Dulworth**
Co-authors of *Reflections of a Stranger* and the Seasons of Change series

A Rifle by The Door is everything you look for in a Western; good versus evil, ranching, gun fights, and a touch of romance. In the spirit of *Shane* by Jack Schaefer, Dan Fuller's gripping coming-of-age story reminds us of the powerful influence one person can have on the life of another.

~**PeggySue Wells**
Bestselling author of *Chasing Sunrise*, *Homeless for the Holidays*, *Slavery in the Land of the Free*, and *The Slave Across the Street*

Fuller draws from a rich heritage of America's greatest Western writers to pen this compelling but unique story. With an attention to deep characters, this novel had me flipping pages to a payoff at the end I'll not soon forget.

~Peter Leavell
Award winning author of West for the Black Hills and Gideon's Call

Acknowledgments

A NOVELIST WORKS in solitude, but the outcome requires a team. I want to thank all those who are my team and cheerleaders. My wife and family-my first line of cheerleaders. Liz and Troy Shockey and Barbara and Edwin Welch who read and typed the second draft of the story. Dr. Dennis Hensley from whom I learned the craft of writing with much encouragement. My fellow writers and friends from the Writers' Bloc at Taylor University and the Marion Writers' Group who critiqued the novel and offered inspiration and advice. Geri Bradford and the computer tech staff at Taylor University. Aubree Devisser who was a great help in teaching me to navigate the business of social media. Terry Burns, western author and agent who did an early edit and guided me through another novel. Head librarian Barbara Dixon and the staff of The Barton Rees Pogue library. Christal Miller for much encouragement and major editing in the final stage.

A special thanks to everyone at Lighthouse Publishing of the Carolinas: Eddie Jones who gave me important advice at a Write-to-Publish Conference, Rowena Kuo and Ann Tatlock who guided me to Jennifer Uhlarik, my editor. Jennifer, thanks for believing in this story and skillfully guiding me through the process of publishing.

Finally and mostly to God, the author of all talents.

Dedication

In memory of my aunt, Orma Miller Fuller, a highly respected secretary and award-winning typist, who saw the potential in this novel, typing the very first draft. And my parents Robert and Mary Fuller, avid readers, who ignited my love for literature and encouraged me to find my own path.

When I was a child, I talked like a child, I thought like a child, I reasoned like a child. When I became a man, I put the ways of childhood behind me. (1 Corinthians 13:11)

Prologue

JOHN BECK RODE into the town, a calm permeating his solitary thought. He would die today.

He was ready.

As he reined his horse onto the main street, he scanned the rutted path. Several people stood on the boardwalks lining the street, some talking to shopkeepers, others packing their purchases into wagons. But as he neared the hitching post outside the mercantile, everything stilled. All conversation stopped, and every eye turned his way.

At the creak of the saloon door, all attention shifted to the man who stepped out—tall, lanky, with grey eyes as frigid as death.

Fallon.

Beck slid from his saddle and, before tying his horse, took a brief instant to loosen his Colt in its holster.

The two men walked toward each other until they were within killing range of their .45's. Fallon pushed his bowler hat back on his head. "Beck, we can just go our ways. You're gettin' too old for this. Slowin' down some."

"Can't." He glanced to the sides and back. "Where's Maxwell?"

"He's already headed for Foster's place."

"Then go for your horse or go for your gun."

Fallon went for his gun, fast as a rattler's strike." The two muzzle blasts exploded so close they sounded like one.

Chapter 1

SOMETIMES IT ONLY takes the scent of pine or a cool breeze coming down off the Rockies, and I am back there in the valley again. I was only thirteen, but I remember it all. The weight of the gun in my hand. The screams of falling horses and dying men. The acrid smell of gun smoke. The stark redness of fresh blood on green grass.

But most of all, I remember … Beck.

#

Southwest Colorado, 1889

Pow! An outlaw went down. Pow! Another one toppled off a cliff. Next, a tomahawk-wielding Indian dropped before the withering fire of my rifle—an aspen stick fishing pole.

"What are you doing?" Pa said, coming up behind me, his expression curious.

"I'm protecting our new ranch from outlaws and Indians."

Pa laughed. "You're more likely to have to defend our stock from insects, disease, and weather." He leaned his rifle against a pine tree.

"All the men have to fight outlaws and Indians out here, Pa."

"Where did you get that idea?"

"It's here in this book." I pulled a dime novel from my back pocket.

Taking the paperback book from my hand, he read the title: *Fighting Cowboys of the Wild West*. "Son, these are just made up stories. Besides, if you ever call a real cowhand a 'cow-*boy*', he might take a shot at you."

"It's what the writer calls them."

"Where did you get this book?"

"In a store back in St. Louis before we started out."

"How much did it cost?"

"Ten cents."

"You spent your hard-earned money for this drivel?"

I hung my head. "Yes, sir." He handed me the book, and I returned it to my pocket.

Pa motioned for me to sit on a boulder beside him. He reached for my fishing pole, looked it over, and laid it across his knees. "The truth is, most people never face any real outlaws in their lifetime, even out here."

I looked at the heavy .44 holstered on his hip. "You carry a pistol."

"Yeah, for rattlesnakes and varmints."

"How about Indians?"

"Without Chief Ouray to help keep the peace, the army pushed most of the Utes onto a reservation in Utah. Those that are left are peaceable folks."

"Aw, shucks."

"No! No. Don't ever be glad about there being no people to kill." Pa snapped the pole in his hands. He glanced at me then looked away, dropping the broken pieces on the ground. "Sorry. I'll cut you another fishing pole tomorrow." He shook his head. "I'm just trying to make you understand, son, it's not like reading a storybook. Men coming at you screaming, falling as you fire and kill, fire and kill." The man stared at the ground. "Then there were the bayonets …"

I looked away, too. "I never thought about it like that."

He paused for several seconds. Removing his hat, he ran his fingers through his hair before putting it back. "David, killing a man in battle is a terrible thing, best avoided if you can help it. Only as a last resort to protect your family, your home, or your country. Or someone who can't defend themselves. A lot of folks found that out during the War Between the States." My father looked off as if looking into the past. "I hope I never have to shoot a man again." His voice grew husky. "I pray to God you never have to." Sadness appeared in his eyes.

I picked up the broken pieces of the fishing pole then dropped them when Pa stood, drew his pistol and fired faster than I had ever seen. A puff of gun smoke irritated my nostrils as it floated on a light breeze. My heart still pounded while he stepped over to another boulder about six feet away and picked up a bloody, headless snake. "That's killing, son." He nodded toward the thing still writhing slightly as it dangled from his hand. "It's ugly and cold and it's forever. You understand?"

"Yes, sir." My voice came out as little more than a whisper. We were silent for an awkward minute after Pa threw the snake into the brush.

I cleared my throat. "You been hunting, Pa?" I nodded toward his Winchester rifle.

Pa seemed to shake off his thoughts and smiled at me. "Yep. Didn't get anything, though. You get any fish?"

"Nope. They weren't biting."

"Probably scared off by all those outlaws you were fighting." He sighed and held up his rifle. "You know, what you will have to shoot is game for the table. Maybe a bear or cougar sometime to protect the stock. If anything ever happens to me, you'll be the man around here. It will be up to you to provide for you and your sister."

"I'm just twelve. Besides, nothing is going to happen to you, Pa."

"The wilderness is often harsh and unpredictable. You'll learn that a fellow has to be prepared for anything. I was helping my father hunt by the time I turned ten." He scratched his chin. "But your mother was tender-hearted and hated guns and killing. That's why I went slow with you. Besides, there wasn't much opportunity to hunt in the city back in Indiana. "But now it's time to start taking on some manly responsibilities around here. So, you want to get in some practice with the real thing? Later this week, we'll go hunting. Maybe you can bring down your first elk."

"Sure!" It was about time. I'd been itching for such experiences for a long while.

"Aim at the small rock on top of that boulder over there." He pointed toward the creek.

The rifle was heavy in my hands, causing the sights to wobble around the target. When I thought I'd lined them up, I pulled the trigger. The gun kicked hard against my shoulder, knocking me backward. I barely stayed on my feet. The smoke cleared, but the rock remained untouched.

"Try again, David. But this time, let your breath out slowly. That will help steady the rifle. Hold the gun tight against your shoulder to ease the kick and squeeze the trigger. Don't pull it."

I rubbed my sore shoulder before levering another shell into the chamber. I held the gun tight against me, then aimed. I let my breath out and gradually squeezed the trigger. The gun kicked again but not so hard. The target rock flew off its stony base.

"That's it, son!" Pa slapped me on the back.

My elation was interrupted by the banging of a spoon against a pan. "Come in, you two. It's time for supper," my sister Jenny called from the porch.

Pa stood and took a deep breath. "I'll never get tired of this mountain air. Makes a man feel bigger just breathing it in. And those snowcapped peaks!" He grinned as if remembering something afar off. "Loved this valley ever since the first time I came out here when I ran freight with John Beck, before I moved back to Indiana and met your mother."

"I wish Ma was here. She would have liked this, too." Grief wound through me as I looked out across our green valley nestled at the foot of the San Juan Mountains. If only the pneumonia hadn't claimed her.

Pa gave a sigh, the sadness returning to his eyes. After a moment, he brightened again. "Come on, son, let's go in. I'm hungry." He put his hand on my shoulder as we walked up the slope. "So, tell me, what do you really want to be when you grow up?"

"I want to be a rancher like you, Pa. Raise the best cattle and horses in the country." I held up the rifle. "And fight outlaws that don't exist!" We laughed together as we walked up to the cabin.

#

Two days later, the first sign of trouble appeared. Pa bought supplies in a one-horse town erroneously named Goldstrike. One day, while he was gone, riders appeared up on the ridge.

"Davy, come here and look at this," Jenny said. She peered out the window. "Earlier today a man was up on the ridge watching our cabin." A nervous edge tightened her voice. "Now there are two. They've been up there for about a half hour just staring. What do you think they're up to?"

"Oh, probably nothing. Just a couple cowpunchers passing between jobs." I shrugged with indifference. Nevertheless, I placed Pa's rifle by the front door where it was handy.

"Maybe they'll come in shooting, and we'll have to fight for our lives. Pow! Pow!" I teased, aiming my arms as if holding the rifle.

"Shut up with that nonsense, and sweep the floor while I finish the dishes." Jenny wiped her hands on the dishtowel, watching the men ride on. Being eighteen, she thought she was my boss.

#

The next day, just after breakfast, trouble stepped out into the open and introduced itself.

"Good morning, my name is Frank Maxwell." The man was tall and wore a long black coat and white Stetson hat. "I own the big ranch in the valley below yours. And this," he indicated a lanky, mean looking rider with a thin growth of beard, "is Mr. Jud Sykes, my overseer." I recognized Sykes as one of the men watching from the ridge a few days earlier.

"I'm Jim Foster, and these are my children, David and Jenny. Why don't you gentlemen step down and sit a spell. There's plenty of chairs on the porch."

Sykes sat and propped one of his boots up on the rung of the chair, his spur cutting into the wood.

"I'll have my daughter fix some coffee." Pa turned toward Jenny.

"That won't be necessary, Foster." Maxwell pulled a big cigar from his coat and lit it. He held another one out to Pa who shook his head. "We won't stay long. I'm a busy man, and I believe in coming right to the point. I moved into this area shortly before you did. I've been buying up land for what will become the biggest cattle and horse ranch in the state."

Pa glanced back at us with an *I know what's coming next* look.

"I would like to buy your land, Foster. I can give you a good price. You name a figure, and we can work something out." With an air of finality, Maxwell flicked what few ashes had collected from the end of his cigar.

Pa didn't pause a second. "Well, Mr. Maxwell, I imagine your offer would be fair. But I've looked forward to living in this particular valley for a long time. I have everything I want here. There's no price that I would take for it."

"You're sure of that?" Maxwell clinched the cigar tight in his teeth.

"Yes. I'm sorry we can't do business, but I think you'll have to expand your land in other directions."

Maxwell's manner turned cold. "Foster, the water from your creek feeds four ranches including mine. That could be a problem for me. I don't want anybody controlling that water except me."

Pa's voice tensed. "I've never withheld water from anybody who needed it, and I don't hold with any man who does. You just stay on your land, and leave me to mine. That's the way we will get along." He cleared his throat. "Now it's time for you to leave."

Maxwell grinned like a Cheshire cat. "Now, now, Mr. Foster, I meant no offense. Dealing in big business as I do, I tend to get in a hurry sometimes and rub folks the wrong way. I'm sure we'll be the best of neighbors. But do think about my offer."

Pa said nothing. The two visitors rose and left the porch. After Maxwell mounted his horse, he looked directly at Pa. "You know this is harsh country. The winters are bitter. There's no law in Goldstrike or within several days' ride from here. And there are ruffians around who would kill you for the money in your pocket. If I can help, come and see me anytime."

Maxwell rode away, but Sykes lingered while he tightened the cinch on his saddle. As he did, he casually slid off the strap that held his pistol in its holster. He swaggered toward my father. "You better talk to Mr. Maxwell about sellin' yer place. Eastern greenhorns never do no good out here. You could git hurt." He spit between gritted teeth.

"Just stay out of this greenhorn's way, sonny." Pa gritted his teeth. No spit.

"A greenhorn that don't know how to handle a gun and goes where he don't belong can die real quick in this country," Sykes' right hand dangled close to his pistol. "You got a real purdy daughter and a fine boy. It'd be a shame if they wuz left all alone and unprotected out here just because they got a stubborn old fool fer a daddy."

Without warning, Pa kicked Sykes' hand away from his gun. Sykes yelped, and Pa slugged him. A flying right cross spun the man off his feet, causing his pistol to fall into the dirt. Then Pa drew his old .44 and aimed it at that dirty, bearded face.

"Now, mister, I try to live a good Christian life, but I believe in defending my family. I won't see them threatened. So, you better follow your trainer back home and stop playing with guns, or you might be the one to get hurt."

Pa picked up the gunman's pistol, unloaded it, and passed it back. With his good hand, Sykes jammed the weapon into its holster, then swung up into his saddle. He held his battered appendage close to his body as he rode away, hate in his eyes.

I beamed at my father. He had to be the toughest man west of the Ohio River. "That was great!" I shouted. "You sure fixed that overseer." I paused a second. "What's an overseer?"

"In this case, son, it means hired killer."

#

The rest of the day carried a solemn air. No one said much. Once Jenny returned from washing the lunch dishes, her voice grew subdued. "Papa,

I think that bearded man, Mr. Sykes, was one of the men who watched us from the ridge the other day."

"I figured as much."

Supper was unusually quiet, and my father's saying of grace was different. "Lord, as always, thank you for this food, your many blessings and … and please protect my family." He smiled as if the last statement was always a part of the evening prayer. "Well, this fried chicken smells delicious. Let's dig in."

The next day, as soon as breakfast was over, Pa rose from the table and put on his coat. "You youngsters take care of the place for a while. I'm going to ride over to Goldstrike and mail a letter."

"Who is it for, Papa?" Jenny looked up as she collected the breakfast plates.

"Just an old friend." He gave no further explanation as he left.

#

"Papa is late," Jenny said, wiping her hands on a dishtowel after cleaning the lunch dishes. "He should be back from town by now."

"He probably found another rancher to talk to, Sis." As time passed, I grew a little uncomfortable myself.

About midafternoon, Jenny looked out the window. "Someone's coming. It's Papa."

I looked out across the valley. "No, Pa took his horse. That fella is in a wagon."

Several minutes later, Joe Warner, owner of the general store, pulled up before our cabin in his big freight wagon. We both gave him pleasant greetings, but he remained silent upon the high seat, the reins dangling loosely in his hands.

"Is something wrong, Joe?" Jenny asked.

"It's yer pa." Joe's voice was quiet, and he wouldn't meet our eyes.

Jenny's spine stiffened. "What happened?"

Joe shook his head. "I've carried bad news before, but it's never been as hard as this."

"Say it, Joe," Jenny commanded, the apprehension rising in her voice.

"One of the miners found yer pa beside the trail. He'd been shot in the back. His money an' horse were gone, everything but that old pistol he always carried."

With strained control Jenny asked the inevitable question. "Is he …?"

Silence answered.

"I've got to go to him," she said, pulling her shawl down from the peg inside the door. "Where is he?"

Silence again.

"Where is he, Joe?" Jenny's voice broke on the edge of hysteria.

Joe nodded toward the back of the wagon.

Both of us hesitated to step to the back and see what it held. Dread churned my stomach. Jenny moved slowly at first, then reached with shaking hands and jerked back the canvas that covered the body in the wagon bed.

I could not cry like her. I stared, anger and embarrassment churning in me at the emotion around me and the lack of it in me.

I said nothing to Jenny or Joe. Just marched into the cabin where I paced around and kicked things, then collapsed in a chair, my head hung toward the floor. A thousand thoughts and memories flashed through my mind, all fogged in darkness, as if I were suddenly cut from my anchor, adrift in a deep and endless sea. In the whole day, I could not force the tears to come. But that night, in the quiet isolation of my room, I could not stop them.

One thought kept slithering into my mind. I wanted to kill the man who murdered my father. And I didn't feel like praying for God's guidance about it.

Chapter 2

THE ONLY OTHER person to attend the simple funeral was Joe Warner. Besides being owner of the general store, he also served as postmaster, doctor, dentist, and the nearest thing to a preacher in the area. His father had been an ordained minister back in Kansas.

As we came down the hill, leaving there a lone wooden marker, Jenny asked, "Davy, what are we going to do now? Papa knew how to survive out here. We don't. The land, the climate, everything is so different from what we're used to."

"We'll make it," I said, trying to sound sure.

"I beg pardon fer breakin' in …" Joe Warner scratched his beard, "Did you folks know about the letter yer pa sent when he was in town?"

"No. Who was it for?" Jenny asked.

"It went to Waco, Texas, the last known address of John Beck."

"John Beck?" I turned to Jenny.

"Papa expected more trouble, I believe." Jenny tilted her head in thought. "Maybe he hoped Mr. Beck would help us."

Joe broke in again. "I wouldn't count on anything but more trouble from a man like Beck. I can't figure how a fine man like yer pa ever knew him."

"Papa mentioned knowing someone named Beck when he lived out here the first time." Jenny looked at me.

I looked up at Joe. "What's wrong with him, Mr. Warner?"

"Well, he's what you call a real western badman. He's a professional gunman. Nobody heard of him until about ten years ago, up in Wyoming, when he walked into a saloon one day and called three men out in a gunfight.

"I was there that day and saw it myself. I remember it like it was yesterday. I was playin' cards with my partner, Bob Ryan. Bob laid down his hand and pushed his chair back from the table.

"'What's wrong?' says I."

"Bob stood and moved toward the wall as he nodded toward the saloon doors. 'Joe, you might want to make some room. That man's come to kill. He's got the look.'"

Joe shook his head. "Well, sir. That day, John Beck called out three tough-lookin' hombres over somthin' he said they took from him. They all went for their guns and started blazin' away. When the smoke cleared, all three of those fellers were dead. Beck was shot up real bad, but he lived. Since then he's done about every kind of job that involves guns and killin'. Cavalry scout, stage guard. He's been a town tamer in places that wanted a fast gun more than a knowledge of the fine points of the law."

"That doesn't sound like the friend Papa told us about." Jenny adjusted her bonnet as a gust of wind caught it.

"Worst of all," continued Joe, "he's turned bounty hunter. Hunting down wanted men for rewards is the meanest work there is, and Beck's one of the best. He don't give up. When he's on a man's trail, that feller's a gone coon as sure as you're born. Why, I've heard tell of growed men cryin' and cussin' at the same time when they learned that John Beck was after them. Yes sir, he always brings them in just like the posters say, *dead or alive* ... but usually dead."

#

The next few weeks were the worst of our lives. Our prayers for help seemed to go unanswered. Preparations had to be made for winter which, we were told, would come early in the high country. We needed to lay in supplies. Chop wood, bring in and cure meat, build and mend corrals and outbuildings. The work was hard, and tempers were short.

I was out hunting on a sun-dappled day, glad to be away from my sister's nagging. A crisp breeze fluttered the pale green aspen leaves as I crossed a shallow stream on my horse, Copper. "Lord, please give me something to take home, so Jenny won't give me a hard time," I prayed silently.

Remembering a small lake I had seen from a hilltop, I turned Copper down a game trail that appeared to head that way. I only went about a hundred yards before the biggest moose I ever saw stepped out of the trees on the slope above me. He probably topped a thousand pounds. His antlers were velvet nubs this early in the year.

The huge beast gazed blankly at me, and I at him. I began to shake. I had no idea how I would get that much meat back home, but I sure would try. Slowly, I drew Pa's rifle from the saddle scabbard. At about 50 yards, it would be an easy shot. The front sight wavered as I tried to hold the gun steady. My heart thumped like a military drum. I pulled the trigger, and the rifle jerked against my shoulder. It knocked me off balance, nearly toppling me from my horse. I dropped the rifle and grabbed onto the saddle horn as Copper ran into the forest, seeming to be in a race with the moose. My hopes turned into the brush with my quarry as I finally got control of my horse and went back for the rifle.

"Is that all you got?" Jenny said with a derisive 'humph' as I presented her with two squirrels that evening. I didn't mention the moose.

#

In the morning, still mad at my sister for questioning my hunting prowess, I saw an opportunity to get back at her. Jenny had taken some clothes down to the creek to wash. As she bent over, I selected an egg-sized rock, took careful aim, and beaned her on the bottom. She yelled and jumped up as she grabbed her backside.

"See? I'm a good hunter," I called. "I just need a wide enough target."

"Oh, you little beast! I'm going to beat you within an inch of your life!"

I laughed as I ran for the outhouse, Jenny right behind me. I slammed the door shut, knowing she wouldn't follow me inside.

"Oh, you're going to get it!"

She settled down as the day passed. Jenny was not one to stay mad very long. At supper that night she was pleasant as usual except that she spilled a cup of water on me. Accidentally … I think.

#

One evening, I whittled on a new fishing pole in the cabin. When Jenny noticed, she whirled from the supper she was preparing. "Get that thing out of here! You're getting wood shavings all over the floor. Besides, you're supposed to be cleaning the shed."

"I already finished it."

"Then go bring in some water."

"I don't have to do everything you say. You're my sister, not my boss."

"You'll know who's boss when I use that fishing pole on your behind!"

I huffed and rolled my eyes.

"Davy, you've got to pull your weight around here if we are going to make it this winter," she pleaded. "I asked you an *hour* ago to bring in that water."

"I shot those three rabbits today for supper, didn't I?"

"A few rabbits are not going to get us through the winter."

"Sorry, but the big game hasn't been accepting invitations to dinner. Since that moose …" I caught myself. "I mean, I don't understand it. I know there are elk and deer around here, but I can't find them. I wonder, since it's summer, maybe they've moved up higher. I'll try the north slope tomorrow. Something is bound to come along pretty soon. Everything will work out. You'll see."

"Oh, sure, everything will be fine. How can you always be so positive? I've never understood that about you. You never worry about anything or get frustrated. You don't stand and fight. You go calmly, playing along, saying that everything will work out in time. You can't be the baby in the family anymore."

I turned away from her and said nothing.

Jenny continued, "Davy, we are running out of time. We are starving to death. I work my fingers to the bone on a garden where nothing grows. All the game has disappeared. I don't know what we are going to do, and I'm getting too tired to care." Tears trickled down her cheeks, but I was too angry to be compassionate.

"You're tired? You try cutting wood half the day, then you'll know what tired is."

Silence.

A set of angry eyes like molten iron glared at me. *Uh oh.* I had stepped into trouble. "But I think I'll go carry in the water, anyway." I left the cabin in a hurry.

All the way back from the creek, sloshing two buckets of water, I complained to myself. "I'm sick and tired of Jenny bossing me around all the time. I just want to go out and play or go fishing. Just be a kid for a little while. It's not fair." But inwardly I knew that Jenny was right. Taking stock of what we had didn't look good. There was the cabin, and an old shed that was here when we arrived. It presently doubled as a stall for my horse, Father's horse that I'd found along the trail, and Jenny's mare. We had a store of food and a little firewood but not enough to last through the coming winter.

I carried the buckets into the cabin and stopped. Jenny stood before the fireplace, looking at a tintype picture of Ma and Pa. She reached up and stroked the picture as if touching their faces. My sister turned to me—glanced at the buckets. Light reflected on her damp cheeks. She spoke in a low, weary voice. "Thanks for bringing the water." Jenny said no more, just turned and went to her room.

I gazed at the picture on the mantel. Our parents looked so young on their wedding day. A lump swelled my throat as a flood of memories washed through my mind. My mother's smile as she placed a fresh pie on the table. Pa laughing as he told a funny story. They were gone, and our world had changed. I did not know it then, but the next day would change my world again, ending my childhood forever. I felt it, though, as I sat and read again the letter that Joe Warner had brought out earlier that day. It read: *I'm coming. Beck.*

Chapter 3

JOHN BECK APPEARED on the ridge above our valley, as silent and threatening as a thunderhead that appears on the horizon before an approaching storm.

It was mid-afternoon, and I waded in the creek, poking under rocks to see what treasures the shallows might hold for a youngster. When I glanced up, a big man upon a tall buckskin horse watched from the ridge maybe a hundred yards beyond the creek. The man sat, unmoving. Indeed, I noticed him only by accident, he seemed such a part of the forest behind him.

There was something ominous about his presence there. Though quite still, he took in everything below with the cold alertness of a hawk. As I watched him, a chill went through me like the breath of winter.

Horse and rider moved down the slope toward me. I ran toward the house, calling, "There's a rider coming in."

Jenny motioned me into the cabin. She leaned Pa's rifle against the doorframe just out of sight and stood, waiting.

The stranger rode into the yard and stopped. Looking through the window, I could see him clearly. He was rough in appearance from his battered tan hat that drooped forward, shading his face, to his worn, dusty boots. His fringed buckskin jacket was dark and worn with long use. Some of the fringes were missing, but those on the right sleeve were neatly trimmed back, I imagined so they would not touch his gun hand, like what I'd read in one of my cowboy stories. But the most striking thing about him was the heavy Colt .45 in a holster slung low on his hip and tied down.

Then there were the hard, sharp features of his face, a face that could have been chipped from the rugged rocks of the mountain behind him. A thick brown mustache curved down and out at the tips like inverted steer horns.

There was no hint of humor or gentleness in his bearing.

"Is this Jim Foster's place?"

"Yes," Jenny answered.

"I'm Beck." His voice was deep and gravel rough. "Your pa sent for me. Now, since everybody knows who's who, you won't need that weapon you've got inside the door."

"How did you know that?" Jenny said, surprise in her voice.

"When I crossed the creek, you kept looking back there to make sure it was in place—even though you probably put it there yourself. You kept your hand on the doorframe, but you weren't leaning on it. Besides," he went on, "if I saw a stranger ridin' in, I would have put a rifle handy myself."

"We got your letter just yesterday," Jenny said.

Beck shook his head. "Could've brought the thing myself and saved the postage."

"You want to come on in?" Jenny nodded toward the door.

Beck stepped down and tied his horse to the hitching rail. Heavy footsteps and clinking spurs rattled on the porch as he approached the door. He was tall with wide shoulders and had to duck a little as he came in. He removed his hat and nodded with cool politeness to Jenny.

"I'm Jenny, and this is my little brother, Davy."

Beck nodded to me.

I hated the fact that Jenny called me *little* brother when we had such an impressive guest in the house. Secretly I planned to get even with her somehow. It wouldn't be the first time I beaned her on the bottom with a rock.

"How did you know our father?" Jenny asked.

"Me and Jim were pards years ago, punching cattle and driving freight. We weren't hardly more than kids then. Met back in the war."

We all looked at each other for a silent, awkward moment.

"So Jim finally got his land. I was with him when we first came across this fine valley. Well, where is he?" The man rubbed his hands and smiled as he glanced around the room.

My sister and I looked at each other, avoiding our guest, hoping someone would say the right words. Finally, Jenny said, "There's a marker up on the hill. You can see it from the yard."

A change came over Beck. There seemed to be a weariness in him. The lines deepened at the edges of his eyes.

"How?" he said.

"Some coward shot him in the back." My reply was edged with bitterness. "We don't know who, but we've got our suspicions."

"I saw the marker, didn't know it was for him." Beck shook his head. "It's funny, you don't see a man for almost twenty years, then miss him by a whisker."

"Papa said you were friends." Softness tinged Jenny's voice.

"I got his letter, and I'm here."

"We never knew what the letter said." I shifted my feet.

"It just said he moved here, and there might be trouble. So, what trouble did you folks git into?" Beck plopped down in a chair Jenny motioned to and dropped his hat on the table.

"Right now, our first problem seems to be getting through the rest of the year." I glanced out the window at the darkening sky. "We haven't been through a winter out here yet. If you could kind of help us get started and maybe give us some pointers, we would be grateful."

"You mean you've been out here less than a year?"

"Yeah. It's been real tough for just Jenny and me."

"How old are you two?"

"I'm eighteen." Jenny nodded toward me. "And Davy is twelve."

Beck rubbed the tip of his mustache between his fingers. "I've got one suggestion. Sell out and go home." He stood. "Neither of you is likely to survive a winter out here. And it will be one tough job for me, wet-nursing two green kids." He cursed under his breath.

"Mr. Beck!" Jenny said, shocked. "I don't care who you are. I will not have foul language in this house. And I'll tell you something else," she went on, "Papa spent half his life dreaming of this place, put his money and sweat in it, and now he's buried under it. We're his family, and we happen to like it here. Besides, we don't have any place else to go. With or without your help we're going to stay, and we're going to make it. So, if you don't want to help, just get on your horse and go back to Texas." The firmness of Jenny's statement surprised me.

"That goes for me too." I squared my shoulders. I really didn't want Beck to leave, but we Fosters stuck together, and I wanted to get my share in.

Beck turned to look at me. For the first time, a hint of a smile played on his face. "Spunky pair, ain'tcha?" He then looked out the back window toward the lone marker on the hill.

The man rubbed his chin. He thought for a long time. "You could make a paying ranch out of this, raise horses or cattle maybe. Have you ever herded stock?"

"A few cows on the farm in Indiana." Jenny looked hopeful.

Beck mumbled something apparently inappropriate under his breath. "You're sure you want to go through with this?"

My sister and I looked at each other, then nodded.

"All right then," Beck said. "I'll expect food, board, and fifteen percent of any money I help you make."

We all agreed.

"Just don't expect a picnic," our new partner said. "First, we have to get ready for winter. You've never seen a real mountain winter before. You may see the first snow in September, but it probably won't stay on the ground until November. From there on you'll have it up to your butts. By midwinter it will often be up to the cabin roof. And don't be surprised if you wake up one morning to find the temperature at forty below. You can take a breath and feel the hair in yer nose freeze stiff. Rough weather may hang on until mid-April. Then you can start getting ready for next winter. You all still game?"

"Yes," we said in unison.

"Well, you sound like you've got sand. We'll see. Now, where's your outhouse?"

"Directly behind the cabin." I spoke up for the group. With that, Beck stepped out the door.

#

"I'm just sick," Jenny said, wringing the towel she held in her hands. "We may have made a terrible mistake. I'm afraid things will be miserable with him here. He's coarse and ill-mannered and uncivilized."

"And dangerous," I said. "But he was a friend of Pa's. If we can overlook his manners, I think he will help us. The fact is, we need his help. We can't make it through the winter as it is. At any rate, I don't think he'll stay long."

Beck didn't return, and Jenny told me to go out and tell him supper would soon be ready. I found him in the shed taking care of his horse. He didn't look around. "Always look after your horse, Dave," he said in his gravelly voice. "It can mean life or death to a man in the mountains."

"Jenny says that supper will be ready soon."

"Good."

He called me Dave. It sounded manly, and I liked that. Nobody in the family thought of me as a man or anything near it. John Beck won my full acceptance in that brief moment.

We all seated ourselves around the table. Beck looked at the pot of stew in the center of the table but waited for someone else to reach first.

"Uh, Mr. Beck," Jenny said. "We always hold hands and pray before eating."

Something akin to shock crossed Beck's face, but he bowed his head with us. His rough hands were so big that Jenny's hand nearly disappeared in his. Afterward, he watched us until we began eating, as if expecting us to pull some other outlandish surprise.

When supper was finished, he sat back with a satisfied expression. "That was a fine meal, Miss Foster. I haven't had better in a long time."

"Thank you, Mr. Beck. My mother taught me." Pride colored my sister's look. "You may call me Jenny."

"Since we'll be together awhile, you all can call me John, or Beck, or whatever you like except ..." He hesitated a second then mumbled, "Never mind, I don't think any of you would use that word anyway."

He got up and started a fire as the evening turned cool with the disappearance of the sun. He sat in Pa's chair. "Care if I smoke?"

"We don't believe in it," Jenny said stiffly, "but you have the freedom to make your own choice, Mr. Beck."

Gazing into the yellow-orange glow of the flames, Beck puffed on a cigarette he'd pulled from his shirt pocket.

We usually sat together in the evening, reading or working on small chores, but it was awkward with Beck there.

Jenny finally broke the silence. "We planned to build a smokehouse next."

"Good," Beck said. "You're all gonna be busy. You've got half as much firewood as you'll need. That old shed out there will have to be finished into a barn, and there's meat to catch."

He got up, pulled his hat off the wall peg, and started toward the door. He then turned back to us. "I made me a bunk in the shed. We all better turn in. It'll be a long day tomorrow. You know, there may not be a one of us see spring, but you're Jim Foster's kids. If you got his kind of grit and pull together and do what I tell you, we'll make it. So, sleep well, children, 'cause tomorrow you grow up."

With that, he was gone.

As I climbed the steps to my bed in the loft, I glanced down over the railing. Jenny sat, silhouetted against the fire, deep in her own thoughts. She would probably be there for a while. Being a thinker, she always tried to consider all angles and possibilities before beginning something new.

A tense excitement bubbled in me as I curled up under my mother's handmade quilt. The world seemed different now because a real western gunman slept a few yards away in our shed.

Restless, I leaned over and opened the window and shutters by my bed. Looking out, I felt a part of the warm security of my high loft and the rich mystery of the wilderness night. The clouds separated enough so the moon glowed in the midst of the sky. The creek became a shining, silver ribbon in the soft light that bathed the earth below.

A hint of movement drew my eye to the forest. A mule deer buck stepped with cautious majesty to the edge of the creek. Easily balancing his great antlers, he lowered his head to drink. After a moment, something caught his attention, and he turned to look off into the distance. Then he bounded effortlessly up the slope and disappeared into the velvet blackness of the forest.

Seconds later, a faint rumble of thunder sounded in the distance. Lightning blossomed just above the horizon at the upper end of the valley. The following thunder rolled closer. The aspen trees beyond the yard swayed and rustled as if something huge and invisible had just moved through them. In a few moments, I felt a cold gust of wind against my face. The moon gave up to the passage of the clouds.

I closed the window and shutters, then nestled back under the covers. Before long I dozed off to the rhythmic brush of pine branches against the cabin and the drowsy patter of rain on the roof. The storm had come to our valley.

Chapter 4

THE FRESH-WASHED FRAGRANCE of the night's rain still lingered in the air of early morning as I stepped out to call Beck to breakfast. I found him washing and shaving by a tree stump next to the shed.

I now noticed little things about him that I had missed before. The breeze blowing his hair revealed a deeply receding hairline. Streaks of gray appeared at the temples. The lines in his face seemed deeper. With his shirt off, the muscles still looked rock-hard, but his body carried the awful scars of numerous battles.

Jenny watched us from the porch. She averted her eyes from Beck's scarred torso as he approached the cabin while pulling on his shirt.

"First thing we'll do is finish that barn," Beck said over breakfast. "We're not gonna be burnin' any daylight until winter comes." He took a swig of coffee. "Be ready for some long workdays."

After breakfast, we headed for the forest. Beck cut suitable trees and trimmed them with an ax. I dragged the logs with a chain hitched to one of the horses. When several stood near the shed, Beck and Jenny cut them to proper size with a cross-cut saw. Jenny was actually pretty good with a saw—for a girl. When she took a break, Beck would have me help with the sawing. At first I kept bending the saw and snagging the teeth in the wood. "Don't push so hard, Dave. Put your strength into the pull," he said. "Then keep up a steady rhythm with me." Soon I had it right.

It was a long day, and my muscles ached. However, pride wound through me at the amount of work we had accomplished. I even felt a kind of comradeship with our stoic partner.

Before he left the house in the evening, he said, "You two did a fair job today. Tomorrow you'll do a little more." And more we did. It seemed that we worked harder every day. Soon Jenny and I grumbled that Beck was the worst of slave drivers. He lacked only a whip, but he didn't need one. He snapped out orders with such cold authority that we never dared refuse.

One day Jenny declared, "I don't know how that old man does it. He drives us like plow horses, but he does as much work as both of us put together and more."

"He makes us look like the old men," I said. "Doesn't he ever get tired?"

Despite our complaints and misgivings, the building phase of our work was soon done. The shed had become a real barn, and the new corral and a smokehouse stood ready for use. Beck, who said little and usually spoke in a cold growl when he did speak, said, "You youngun's did real good." If pride could be measured in time and inches, I would have been ten years older and a foot taller. I could tell Jenny felt the same.

After supper Beck got up and stretched. "Tomorrow, we're gonna take a day off. Seeing how it's Sunday, I reckon that will please you, Jenny."

"Yes!" She clapped her hands. "Besides I feel like I can use a change, too, after feeding and cleaning up after you two. And doctoring all the bruises and skinned knuckles you've gotten from those logs. A few of my own, too." She rubbed her hand.

Beck shared one of his rare smiles.

"I almost forgot it was Sunday," she continued. "We'll have to have a prayer service before breakfast."

"You mean you have to do it every Sunday morning no matter what?" Beck said with a hint of displeasure.

"The Sabbath is to be recognized as a holy day, Mr. Beck," Jenny said.

"And a day of rest," he reminded her.

#

Beck didn't appear until breakfast the next morning and seemed inclined to do little the rest of the day but eat and lounge about the cabin and the yard. Just once, shortly before noon, I noticed him standing on the hill by the grave. He looked rather lonely there, lost in his own world of thoughts. I doubted then that we would ever really know him well.

After lunch, Jenny persuaded us all to take a walk up on the mountain. We came to a clearing far up on the slope. From there we could see the whole valley. The cabin looked like a toy house of twigs below us. Jenny, Beck, and I lingered in the clearing. He lay back against a log to take a snooze in the warm sun. Jenny stood looking out across the valley. A light breeze billowed her hair.

Eventually, she noticed that Beck watched her. She turned to him, smiling. "I love the wind in my face and the fragrance of the air. It's so beautiful here. I can understand why Papa loved it so. It's like a storybook world. The mountains remind me of great castles."

"I reckon a handsome prince will come to take you away to be his bride," Beck said.

"Yes! Only I suppose he'll be wearing a Stetson hat and chaps instead of armor." She laughed.

Once again, the shadow of a smile touched his hard features.

Jenny sat on the end of the log and thought for a moment. Finally, she asked, "John, do you believe in God?"

Beck shrugged, "Life and all the world's a great mystery. Who knows who started the whole dang thing?" he said.

"Will you please stop using that kind of language!" Jenny said with exasperation. "I can tell you, John Beck, that it started with a mind far greater than ours that will not tolerate such language or disrespect."

"Now look, when trouble hit me in the face, I didn't see nobody step down from the sky to do me any favors. So, if you're planning to preach, little girl, you better save it for somebody that can use it."

"We seldom see miracles, *Mr. Beck*, when we refuse to look!" Jenny pushed back a lock of hair and cleared her throat. "You have a right to your opinions, of course. But someday you may find yourself crying out to that One that you scoff at so easily." With that, she marched off.

Beck watched her walk away. I could not decipher the meaning of the expression on his face.

Chapter 5

WE KNEW BECK had a violent past. We did not know that it would follow him to our front door.

I remember it especially well because it happened the same night that I learned the evils of smoking. We'd just finished supper. Jenny cleared away the dishes while Beck finished his last cup of coffee. I sat by the fire looking over some unusual rocks I had collected from the creek.

After finishing the dishes, Jenny went into her room. Beck came over by the fire and sat down in the rocking chair. After searching all his pockets, he pulled out a wrinkled piece of paper and a small cloth bag. Pouring what little tobacco that remained in the pouch onto the paper, he rolled the paper around the tobacco and licked one edge over the other, sealing it all into a limp, battered-looking tube. Then taking a burning twig from the fire, he lit it, inhaling the smoke. After a moment he exhaled a foggy cloud that floated above his head then dissipated into the air.

I had seen men roll cigarettes before but not up close. I watched the red glow at the tip fade into gray ash. The longer I watched, the more curious I became. Finally, I asked, "Do cigarettes taste good?"

"Nope."

"What do they taste like?"

"Burnt buffalo chips."

Well, I knew what buffalo chips were, and smoking the leavings of those shaggy beasts did not sound at all inviting. Yet, my curiosity remained, so I asked, "Why do you smoke them?"

"It's a habit, boy. A habit's a hard thing to break. Y' see, when I was a little shaver, not as old as you, I thought smoking was a real growed up thing, and it'd make me a man if I did it. Maybe like what you're thinking right now."

Beck leaned back and took another draw on the cigarette, then blew out the smoke in a big puff. "Well, sir," he continued, "smoking never did a thing for me, but once I got started, I just kept doing it without hardly thinking about it. That's the way habits can do you." He stared at the glowing tip an instant before looking at me. "Remember, Dave, be careful about the habits you pick up. If a fella don't watch, they can be the death of him. Why, I knew a man named Bill down in Texas that got in the habit of teasing rattlesnakes."

Now I was really fascinated. "Tell me about that."

"Well, Bill wouldn't shoot a snake. He'd tease at it with a stick until it was all hissing and rattling mad. Then he'd wave his hat in front of its nose. Just when the snake was ready to strike at the hat, Bill would reach around, grab the critter by its tail, and swing it around his head, a hootin' and hollerin' like an injun. After a while he'd smash its head on a rock and skin the thing to make fancy belts and other googaws. Folks kept saying, 'Bill, you're going to get yourself killed, playing with rattlesnakes.' But, Bill couldn't quit. He had the habit. He had to keep trying just one more snake."

"What happened to him?"

"One day he got himself killed."

I thought over the story for a moment. "I heard that you can cut out the poison."

"He tried, but that rattler was a big monster, and it hung on too long. It was just too much for Bill. When his partner brought him in, he was all blowed up like a dead toad that's been laying in the sun."

I sat quiet for a while, picturing the ghastly images Beck had just created in my mind. Then I got back to my original purpose. I looked around to make sure Jenny was still in her room. The moment seemed right, so I asked, "John, can I try it?"

"Try what?"

"A puff on a cigarette."

He thought for a moment, then took the one out of his mouth and handed it to me.

"I was hoping for a fresh one."

"Nope, that's my last one. Take it or leave it."

The sight of that wet, well-chewed stub revolted me. But there seemed to be no time for debate, so I took it.

"Now you do it right when you do it," Beck said. "You draw in a long, deep breath. Remember, that's the trick, breathe deep, and fill your lungs."

I did as he said. Suddenly the world turned to smoke and fire. My lungs burned and ached for air. I gasped, choked, and sputtered with smoke rolling out of my mouth and nostrils like dragon's breath. That ended any desire to try smoking again.

Through it all, I could hear Beck's restrained chuckles. "You're doing fine, Dave. How do you like it?" he said with mock sincerity. He gave me a hearty slap on the back that brought on another fit of coughing.

Before I could answer, Jenny came storming into the room. "John Beck, what are you doing to that child?" She grabbed the cigarette from me and threw it into the fireplace.

"There ain't no harm done." Beck worked to hold in another chuckle.

"No harm! Davy is a growing boy. I don't want you fostering such bad habits on this ..."

"Shut up," Beck said.

"What?" Jenny gasped in shock.

"Be quiet. Listen." Beck watched the door, his eyes narrowed as if searching for something yet unseen. After several tense and silent moments, the faint sound of a horse neighing echoed in the distance. A moment later the muted clink of a spur jangled as someone stepped onto the porch.

"Everybody move to the corners of the room and keep down," Beck whispered as he stepped toward his pistol hanging on the opposite wall. He stopped by the table to blow out the lantern where it hung from the ceiling.

Just as he lifted it down, the front door burst open, sending splinters of the broken latch flying into the room. In the doorway stood a huge, bearded man with a double-barreled scattergun. "Beck!" he yelled as he leveled the awful weapon.

With lightning reflexes, Beck flung the lantern at his assailant as the man brought up the shotgun. The lantern crashed against the man's chest and burst into flames, sending him, reeling, back onto the porch. Jenny screamed as the shotgun went off toward the ceiling with a deafening roar. Acrid smoke fogged the air.

Beck leaped across the smoke filled room. He yanked his pistol from its holster and fired through the doorway. The bearded man, yelling and cursing, his shirt aflame, staggered backward but struggled to bring up the shotgun for a second shot. The pistol flashed as Beck fired again. The bearded man jerked backward and fell off the porch.

As suddenly as it began, the battle ended. We could see nothing of the dead man except for an eerie glow beyond the porch. But the acrid smell of burning cloth and flesh hung heavy in the air, reminding us he was still there. Beck went out and closed the door behind him. We never saw the corpse again nor the place where Beck buried him.

I lit a lantern and looked around at my sister. "Are you all right?"

She nodded but remained silent. After a few minutes she said, "I've got to clean up this place." She worked furiously around the room, although everything looked as neat as it ever had except for a chair that had been knocked over in the scramble and the splinters hanging from the ceiling that had received the blast of the shotgun. Yet, she dusted everything and swept the floor, brushing the dust into the fireplace, avoiding getting close to the front door.

"Who do you think that man was?" I glanced back at the door.

"I don't know."

A crash brought me around. Jenny stood over the shattered pieces of a coffee cup. Her hands shook, and she tried hard to fight back the tears that coursed down her cheeks.

"Davy, we've got to tell him to leave. We've got to make him go away. I cannot live with a killer on this property."

"Sis, the man tried to kill him. Beck had to defend himself."

"Violence and death have come here because of him! You've got to stand with me to make him go. If you don't, who knows how many murderers he will attract here?"

"Maybe you don't think I will, Jenny, but I will stand up to John Beck or whoever I have to when it's necessary. Right now, it's necessary for him to stay." My words sounded firmer to me than my voice. "Look, you know how it was before he arrived. We could hardly keep food on the table. Since he's come, we've learned a lot about how to survive out here. He's worked hard, and he's always been honest with us. You'll have to admit that he has also been polite to you—most of the time."

My sister raised an eyebrow at that statement.

"Jenny …" I hesitated before I offered my next thought. "The man that killed Pa is still out there. It's possible that he might come after us … and I sure can't fight or shoot like John Beck."

Jenny glanced at me, eyes wide. She turned away and thought a minute then turned back to face me. "I know," she said. "But John is godless and coarse and violent. He is teaching you bad habits, and who knows what immoral stories and bragging you've picked up from him."

"He hasn't told me any bad stories. Well, not too bad anyway."

"Don't you understand, Davy? He's changing us. He's changing what we think and believe and what we are. We may see the day when we're no longer moved by seeing a man killed on our front steps. I pray that day never happens."

"It won't," I said. "When spring comes, and we've learned enough to take care of ourselves, and it looks like we're safe, I'll tell him it's time to leave. I promise. But for the next few months, we'll have to keep him on and put up with his ways."

Jenny thought for a few minutes then, with a hint of surrender in her voice, she said, "All right, I'll tolerate him until spring. But I expect everyone in this family to stick to all teachings of our parents and the Bible. I'm oldest, and without Momma and Papa, I'm responsible for both of us. Don't you see? I must be strong. I can't give in. I can't let him change us. I can't." Her hand clenched tightly again, and she still fought against the tears.

Beck came back in. He looked at us and asked, "Is everybody all right?"

"Yes," I answered, glancing at Jenny.

"I reckon you'll be wanting to know who that was. His name was Jack Riley. I took his brother in to be hung for bank robbery and murder down in New Mexico. Jack swore he'd git me for it.

"I always kinda figured Jack was in on that bank job, but he was never identified. Jack had more grit than his brother. He said he'd kill me ... He tried."

Beck then turned to Jenny. "I'm sorry you and the boy had to see it. A killing ain't a proper thing for women and youngsters to see. It happens sometimes, though."

"I hope it doesn't happen again," Jenny said without looking up at Beck. "If you will all excuse me, I think I'll go to bed now." Without saying anything more, Jenny went to her room, picking up the family Bible from the mantel as she passed.

Beck went out to his room in the barn. He seemed unbothered by having just killed a man. Yet, I sensed a change in him. He was darker and more distant than ever. It was a mood—an instant readiness for violence that I would see again very soon.

My sister and I also felt the change coming over us after that night, especially Jenny. Living with a hard man in a hard land made us stronger, more independent. Yet, we were losing something dear and delicate that could never be regained. We were losing our innocence.

Chapter 6

OCCASIONALLY, BECK WOULD ride away for hours at a time. We never asked where he went, and he never offered an explanation. Once, after he came back, I made a mistake that almost cost me my life.

Jenny and I were out picking berries, and I returned to get another pan. Beck had just put his horse in the barn and headed out the door. On a childish whim, I decided to see if I could scare the big man. I sneaked to the corner of the barn, and just as he passed by, I jumped out and yelled, "Hey!"

In one explosive motion, Beck whirled, drew, cocked, and aimed his pistol directly at my face.

My whole world focused on the end of that gun barrel. Its wide, black hole gaped at me. I froze tight. Seconds ticked by before I could even shake with fear.

Shock and anger mixed in Beck's eyes. He jammed the gun into its holster and charged forward. He grabbed me by the shirt and shook me like a dog shakes a rat. "Don't you ever, ever do that again! You stupid brat. You know you were one split second from being dead? Dead! Do you understand that? I almost blew your brains all over the barnyard."

The tension in him seemed to ease a bit, and I broke loose, running behind the barn. It took effort to hold back the sickness that welled up along with my tears. I was hurt but mostly ashamed because I had done something that made me small in John Beck's sight. No more miserable creature could be found on earth. I hated myself, and I hated Beck.

After several minutes, he came around the corner and looked at me where I sat on the woodpile. I couldn't look back at him or speak. He didn't say anything for a long time, either. Finally, he said, "Well, you sure gave me a start. I reckon I shouldn't have yelled at you like I did, even though you deserved it. Everybody knew what I was before I came here. But being ready to use this gun at any second is the way I've stayed alive for the last ten years. When I'm jumped, I go for it. That's the way it is.

"Had a feeling something like this might happen someday, and I'd end up killing the wrong person. Saw a man kill his best friend that way once. I wouldn't want it to happen with you and me." He paused again. "Anyway, I'm sorry." Pain filled his eyes as he glanced at me, but I still could not respond.

He disappeared into the barn and came back with three empty horse liniment bottles. Placing these on the top rail of the corral, he came back by me. "Maybe it's time you see what guns are really about." Before I caught the movement, the pistol was in his hand and three quick shots blew the bottles to pieces.

"Guns are made for no other reason than to kill, Dave. As long as men are both bad and good, they'll be doing that to each other." He pointed to the shattered bottles. "It ain't a good thing, but that's the way it is. In the wilderness you have to live around guns, so treat them with caution, and never take a man lightly who carries one."

"Can I hold it?" I asked, my voice almost a whisper. After a moment's thought, he removed the bullets and handed it to me. It was big and heavy, almost as heavy as Pa's old army pistol. I had to stretch out my finger to reach the trigger.

"There aren't any notches on it," I said.

"Business with a gun is no game where you gotta count up points." Taking the pistol back, he reloaded it.

As he turned to leave, I said, "I'm sorry about a little while ago."

To that he just nodded and disappeared around the corner. Nothing else was ever said about the incident.

#

The next time Beck's association with guns came up, it was from me asking questions again. We chopped and stacked the last of the firewood with which we would challenge the bitter assault of winter. Beck wore his Colt .45 as usual. A short leather thong over the hammer kept it from slipping out of the holster except when he thought he might need it, which was anytime but when he was riding or sleeping. On the few occasions he didn't wear the pistol, he kept it or his Winchester rifle close by.

"John, are you a western 'badman'? A gunfighter? That's what Joe Warner said."

Beck gave me a curious look. "Bad man? I suppose. Not as bad as some men. Not near as good as some others like your pa. He was a good man. One of the best."

We both sat silent for a moment before he went on. "Gunfighter? Well, I haven't heard that word before. Must be some Eastern term in one of those dime novels. Folks out here call a man who's good with a gun, a gunman or shootist or gun-hand. In Spanish, he's a pistolero. I guess that's what I am." He heaved a breath. "Didn't plan it that way, but I reckon that's the way it turned out. One time some men took something important from me. By the time I caught up with them, I didn't have a job or a home anymore, just a reputation that wouldn't go away. Ever since that day, I've been going after the same kind of men—thieves, murderers, scum ... all of them. I keep bringing them in, but they keep springing up like weeds in a garden." He didn't say anything more but continued chopping with more vehemence.

I also remained silent as we worked, but I wondered what it would really be like to kill a man. Not so long ago, I was playing cowboy and shooting imaginary outlaws with a stick. It seemed exciting. After what I'd seen since Beck came, I had different thoughts. It wasn't a game. It was frightening and sad. Pistols still intrigued me, but not in the same way anymore. A chill swept me at the thought of using one against another person. A chill like a shadow passing over my soul.

Chapter 7

AT BREAKFAST, BECK announced that we would all saddle up and take a ride. "I want to show you both something that's gonna make us a little money."

With great curiosity, we followed Beck into the hills. After an hour's travel, Beck halted us at the top of a ridge. Below was a clearing in a valley. On the other side, a thick cover of aspen and pine trees reached up into the mountains.

Beck sat still as a rock, watching the scene before us. Jenny and I followed his example. Tension grew in me as I wondered what we waited for. Finally, movement within the trees at the far end of the valley drew my attention, and a big gray horse stepped into the clearing. He stood there looking noble, silhouetted against the green slopes. He stamped one forefoot and looked all around before turning back and giving a shrill whinny. Immediately a faint rumble of hoof beats followed and a dozen mares joined their leader.

"They're wild as a mountain storm," whispered Beck. "I first saw them here a couple days ago. They like to water at a stream that runs through a canyon over yonder. If we can block off one end and run those broomtails into it, we can bar the near end and catch ourselves some horses. I used to know a fella over in Telluride who would pay a fair to middlin' price for half broke horses."

The horses had spread out now and contentedly cropped grass. They presented a serene picture, wandering about the clearing. But they were wild as deer. Most of them, mares, daughters of wild mustangs, were descendants of a long line stretching back to the days of the Spanish explorers. They, like their leader, had gracefully arched necks that ended in a head with a roman nose that made them look more horsey than the few domestic mares that had been lured away from nearby ranches to join this free herd. Looks were deceiving, though. The truly wild ones were as wily and skilled at survival as coyotes.

That afternoon, we went to the canyon with axes and ropes, cut down small trees, and blocked one end of the canyon. Then we made a makeshift fence at the other end, leaving a wide gap for the horses to pass through. Beck trimmed saplings, making poles to slide across the opening to close in our captives. Beck was trimming a pole with a large, mean looking Bowie knife he carried in a sheath attached to his saddle. When I asked him about it, he said, "Well, I'm just kinda' partial to the thing. It's brought me through some tight spots."

A mischievous twinkle glinted in his eye. "Did I tell you about the time your pa and me were trapped in a box canyon by a pack o' wolves?" At my negative reply, he went on. "Well, we were camped in a pine canyon up north in Montana. It was a December night, blacker than pitch and colder than a tart's heart."

"What's a tart?" I asked

"Uh, well." Beck cleared his throat. He had a funny look on his face. "It's … It's a woman with a cold heart. That's enough to know for now."

Beck went on with his story. "Anyway, all of a sudden, we heard a long, lonesome howl off in the woods. Then another. Pretty soon, they were all around us. Wolves, thirty or forty of 'em, hungry as starved grizzlies and near as big. They charged in howlin' and growlin' as they came." He paused in his work to pin me with a glance. "Well, sir, it was so cold our guns froze up and wouldn't fire. So we had to fight 'em with our knives and axes. One big monster jumped me from behind—he must have weighed two hundred pounds. He had me down and was about to rip out the back of my neck."

A creeping chill stole up my spine. I listened with wide-eyed fascination to Beck's story.

"Just then yer pa grabbed up Mr. Bowie here," he said, patting the big knife, "and killed that wolf. Near split him in two. Saved me from getting et right there on the spot."

Beck then shook his head and sighed. "It was a waste of time, though. There was too many of them. We couldn't fight them all off."

"How did you get out?" I asked, my heart thumping.

"We didn't, boy. They killed and et us!"

As he laughed I kicked at a rock in disgust. "Aw, that joke's older than I am."

"That sure makes it real old, don't it," he said, still looking amused at my gullibility.

"Pa did tell us a similar story about being cornered by Indians. But he said you saved his life."

"He was just being modest." Beck turned to me, his expression serious. "Your pa was the bravest man I ever met. And he always treated everybody fair."

It made me feel good to hear that about Pa, and I felt closer to Beck, too. For hours I imagined all sorts of adventures about them working and fighting side by side before I fell asleep that night.

#

The next morning, we rode out early again to the place where we first spotted the wild herd. They were not in the clearing, so we stayed out of sight and rode to the top of a hill. I watched the rim of the valley, expecting to see the mustangs come galloping into view at any moment.

We still didn't see our quarry until Beck pointed off to the right. There, far down in the valley, several small, dark objects moved away from us. "They've already headed for the stream," Beck said. "Dave, you work your way over to the left, but stay in earshot. When you hear me, yell and take out after those animals like your pants are on fire. Make a lot of noise and wave your rope. Jenny, take the right. We want them too scared to stop running until they know they're caught."

We rode cautiously just out of sight of the mustangs until Beck decided we were close enough. He yelled, "Hyah!" Then everything on four legs broke and ran. Though I went so fast I thought I would be blown off my horse, I couldn't keep up with John Beck. He was magnificent, as wild and bold as the beasts he pursued, flying after them with blood curdling rebel yells. A picture of the untamed boldness of the West that I imagined from all the dime novels I'd ever read.

That same exhilaration filled me as my own horse pounded the ground below me, the wind blowing in my face. I yelled with all my might and waved my rope. It was all I could do to hang on, but I would not have slowed down for all the gold in California.

Half hidden in great clouds of dust, the horses thundered into the canyon. They didn't stop until they found their escape blocked by logs and brush. Beck jumped down from his mount and yanked poles across the opening. The mustangs were ours!

#

Beck had his own methods of breaking horses. When the mustangs were ready to be brought to the ranch, he roped the leader and dragged him home behind his own horse. The others followed with Jenny and me urging them on from behind.

We turned the horses into the large corral, and Beck cut one out and herded it into the smaller pen. There he roped it, planted his feet firmly, and held on.

The stocky, black mare seemed to be one of the wildest of the lot, and there was a fierce look in her eyes. She didn't appreciate that rope at all. Though she fought it savagely, Beck, by brute strength and force of will, worked the beast over to the snubbing post.

Once securely tied, the horse settled down somewhat. Beck continuously talked to her in gentle, soothing tones. The words, however, did not complement the tone, being unfit for any creature that could understand them. Then the man introduced the horse to its saddle and blanket. He held them before the horse until the animal became used to them. Slowly he placed the saddle blanket on the horse's back. The blanket wasn't too offensive, so the horse waited. Beck followed the same procedure with the saddle. He went through the process with both objects several times. Coming back to the fence, Beck said, "She's taken the equipment pretty well, but I don't like the look in her eye. I think she's planning something outrageous. But I got a couple tricks for her too."

Jenny and I watched as Beck went back to the horse. He used a short rope instead of reins and loosened the rope that held her to the post. When he tried to step up into the saddle the animal jerked and tried to kick him, so Beck continued speaking with a gentle patter until he was close enough to reach her ear. He pulled the ear down and bit it savagely. The horse tensed against the sudden pain, and before she realized it, Beck swung into the saddle.

What happened next I'll never forget. The mare arched her back and shot into the air like a tin can blown off a firecracker. She came down with a jolt. After that, she bucked; she whirled, she danced, and tried every trick she knew. Yet, Beck stayed on as if glued. When the mare slowed down to catch her breath Beck jumped off. At that moment, the horse jerked again and Beck landed bottom side first, exploding a cloud of dust around him. He went through the procedure a couple more times until the mustang began to tire.

Beck walked stiffly to the fence and looked at us sitting on the top rail. "You're next," he announced to me. "I softened her up for you."

I looked with apprehension at the horse, which still pranced around the corral. "How do you expect me to stay on something like that?"

"You gotta balance your weight against her moves. When she goes forward, you lean back. If she goes back, you lean forward and so on. And don't pull leather. Try to keep one hand free all the time. You'll get the hang of it after eating grass a few times."

"What do you mean, eating grass?" I asked with a raised eyebrow.

"You'll find out."

"John, you can't ask my little brother to ride that horse. He's too young. He might get hurt," Jenny said.

"Look, if you two are going to handle ranching after I'm gone, you're both going to have to do the hard jobs that are a part of it. I got throwed off my first horse when I was about Dave's age."

It riled me that Jenny still called me *little brother* and thought I couldn't do anything. "I'll ride," I said, now more determined than ever.

Beck held the horse while I mounted. The mare that had seemed rather small grew incredibly tall. The ground looked a long distance away from the top of the saddle. The horse seemed momentarily confused by my lighter weight on her back, but she only paused a moment. Then she ducked her head and threw her rump into the air. I followed the back end. To my horror the clouds came nearer. I somersaulted over the horse's head and landed on my feet—sort of—and toppled over on my face. Beck looked down at my dusty face and said, "That's called eating grass."

Chaos surrounded me. Jenny flew to me, screaming. Everyone stood around yelling and asking me questions, but I was fully aware only of the pain and empty feeling inside as I gasped for air.

"He's all right," said Beck. "Just had the wind knocked out of him."

"How could you put him on a wild animal like that?" Jenny accused.

"He's not hurt. Are you, son?"

I would have answered, but I still wheezed and spit out dirt.

"Okay, kid," said Beck, brushing me off. "Show that horse who's boss."

"He's just a child!" Jenny stomped her foot.

"Everybody quit it!" I spit out some more dust. "I'm not a child. And I'm not getting back on that stupid horse to break my neck. I'm through. I quit." With that I marched toward the cabin.

"Dave." Beck's voice stopped me. I turned back and looked at the tall man. At that moment, the world lay empty except for him and me, and the truth.

"Dave, you're hurt, and mad, and scared to get back in that saddle. Nobody said it's easy being a rancher or a man. But I know this. If you don't get back on now, you won't ever want to try again. The longer you wait, the harder it'll be. Until you do, fear will be your boss. If you try again, then walk away, you'll know you beat the fear. And you'll know you can do it again when you have to."

The last thing I wanted to do was remount that snorting beast. But I believed what Beck said, and I knew he was right about me. I was scared. I thought a long time. Finally, I slapped my hat against my dusty pants and went back into the corral.

As Beck held the mare, I climbed back up on that four-legged tornado. I could feel the horse tense up between my legs as I clamped them tight. My nostrils filled with the pungent odor of horse sweat and saddle leather while I held the reins tight in my fists. This time, I tried to concentrate on my balance. I stayed on three or four long seconds before being thrown again. I hit easier too, receiving only a couple more bruises. I grabbed up my hat from the ground and marched past Beck without saying a word.

"You did good, Dave. You'll make a man, all right," Beck said.

I huffed as I stomped back to the cabin, glad the ordeal was over but feeling kind of proud of myself.

#

Day after day, the horse-breaking continued. We worked hard, but Beck always did the major part, taking first crack at each horse and working longest with the tougher animals, always wearing them down for me. I even found myself riding without being pressured. Beck saved the easiest and tiredest for me until my skill grew. The landings seemed to be getting easier, and I got thrown less often. It was just the beginning of all the things, wondrous and dangerous, that came with being a rancher.

Chapter 8

As OUR LIVES changed, daily it seemed, we changed. We were becoming experienced ranchers. Jenny complained that I was growing out of my clothes, and it would cost a fortune to keep me in boots. Even Beck seemed to mellow somewhat, becoming more relaxed as the days grew shorter with the approaching crispness of autumn. Yet, somewhere beneath lay that element of cold alertness and danger that was a part of him. A hidden violence that might still one day explode.

Jenny seemed to change the least. Jenny was, well … Jenny. That is until one afternoon I noticed Beck watching her from the corral. She stood barefooted, hanging some clothes on the line. The wind pressed her blouse tight against her body and fluttered her skirt above her ankles. "I'm afraid trouble's coming, my friend," Beck said with a sigh and a shake of his head.

"What do you mean?"

"Your sister's in bloom. Come spring, there'll be so many young men around here wanting to pay attention to Jenny, we'll have to keep the shotgun cleaned and ready every minute."

"You mean men will be coming around to court Jenny?" I asked with disbelief.

"Sure, she's not a child anymore. She's becoming a fine-looking woman."

I always thought Jenny was pretty, kind of like Ma, but the thought that men might actually be interested in her never occurred to me. "I never expected that. I'm sure never going to get married. I don't know what people see in it anyway."

"Well, you'll change your mind someday, and that's one of the facts of life."

"Facts of life? What are those?"

Beck glanced at me with a strange look.

"Well, uh ... How old did you say you are?"

"Twelve."

"And nobody ever told you about marrying and babies and such?"

"Well, Pa did some, but not all the details. I've heard talk."

He looked out over the creek, then he shook his head. "I sure never figured I'd ever be doing this. Come on, let's take a walk."

As we walked along the creek, he said, "You grew up on a farm. You know how animal babies get made. That's the facts of life. It's not so different with people."

"Oh, sure, I know that. But there's got to be some differences in the details between men and women and animals."

"That sure is true, though, some people don't act like it. A marrying kind of love is more than just what feels good. It's caring about another person to where her needs and well-being become more important to you than your own. When a man and woman both love each other like that, it's going to be a good marriage. The children that come from it will have good examples to grow up to. You know, like your ma and pa."

"John?" My nerves tensed up, and my hands shook as I approached another thought that worried me. "I ... Well ..."

"Spit it out, boy. If you've got something that needs saying, don't fiddle-foot around about it."

"When I was in school last year, a boy brought a tin-type picture that he got from his older brother. I don't know where he got it. I didn't know what it was until I looked at it. Well, it showed a lady lying on a fancy couch."

"And?"

I cleared my throat. "She didn't have hardly any clothes on." It seemed necessary to clear my throat again. "Just a couple nights ago, I dreamed about that picture. The lady turned real. She smiled all friendly like and walked toward me. Then I woke up all in a sweat. What does that mean?"

"That, my boy, just means that you're becoming growed up. Every man goes through it."

"Is it a sin to have those dreams?"

"No. Nobody can control what they see in a dream. The wrong there, as I see it, is people showing off private things for money and those who get them to do it. The thing to remember is that a girl ain't no cow or horse. A girl isn't just there to serve your purposes, then you walk away. When you find a woman you love, she deserves your respect and protection, sometimes even from your own selfish or bad habits."

Beck looked off across the valley. "This can be a hard world on women, especially out here. Though I got to admit, these western ladies are strong people. Still, they're not physically as strong as men in a place where there's very physical dangers. Every woman deserves a man's respect and protection."

Beck thought a moment then added, "That includes your sister. Like not bad-mouthing her or throwing rocks as I saw you about to do the other day."

I sighed. "Yes, sir."

Beck stopped to throw a pebble into the creek. "I remember the first time I really knew how much I loved my wife."

John Beck was married? There was news that raised my eyebrows. I never pictured him as being anything but alone.

Beck continued, "I looked out the cabin window and saw her sitting by the river, dabbling her feet in the water. She seemed peaceful and happy. She looked so small out there in the middle of all that rough, vast country. I realized right then and there that what I wanted more than anything else in the world was to care for her and keep her safe."

Beck gazed off into the distance. "Yes, sir, it's a fine feeling when a fella stands on his own land in the early morning and looks back at his house, knowing his family is warm and safe. I just wish I'd ..."

Beck's expression turned dark. "That was a long time ago." He picked up a larger rock and threw it hard, far out into the water.

He remained silent for some time, then shook off his thoughts. "Dave, treat every woman like a lady, decent, whoever or whatever kind she might be, and you'll both be better people for it. Jenny's time is near for the things of a grown person like marrying and creating new life. Your time will come, too."

Beck walked back toward the cabin, leaving me kind of excited but a little bit afraid, like I stood on the edge of a great ocean about to begin a journey to an unknown land.

Chapter 9

THE TIME CAME to take the horses to Telluride, but Beck told Jenny that it would be best for her to stay home.

"Why can't I go? I helped work with those horses right along with you and Davy."

"Because somebody has to stay here and look after the place," Beck said.

"This place will be just fine without me for a couple of days."

"Yeah, but this will be rough riding through high, rugged country. Too hard for a girl."

"Girl?"

"Woman. Anyway, it won't be no buggy ride."

"John, you said yourself that if we are to become ranchers, we've got to learn to do the tough jobs."

"Well, what about your garden? Don't it need tending?"

"I have most of my canning done already. The rest can wait."

Beck hesitated. "Well …"

"I need to get away from here and see some real stores besides that little box Joe Warner runs. I'll be fine. How much could go wrong between here and there anyway? Besides, you'll be with us."

Beck looked as if he could think of a hundred possible tragedies. He hesitated for a moment, then looked at Jenny. "All right, but I don't want to hear any complaining from you when things git tough out on the trail."

"Thank you, John. I'll go pack right now." Jenny walked toward the cabin and then turned back with a smile. "I knew you'd give in." She scurried into the cabin.

Beck rolled his eyes and looked at me. I just shrugged.

#

A special feeling came with traveling the wild country so big and wide, and we three riders so small. As we worked down into lower elevations, the trees became more sparse and the temperature warmer. The rolling land reminded me of the prairies we first crossed, but the mountains remained in view. We camped the first evening by a fast-running stream, moonlight shimmering upon its rippling surface. The air was colder now that we had climbed to high ground again. The warm flicker of a fire and rich aroma of strong coffee were never so inviting.

The red golden glow of the fire danced upon Beck's deep lined face as he stared into the flames and talked of earlier days. "I drifted a lot, never stayed at one job too long. I drove cattle mostly and did some prospecting with yer pa. Matter of fact, we did a little mining up near Telluride where we're headed now."

"Why did you give up mining?" Jenny sipped her coffee.

"We had to hunt and scratch too hard to find anything worthwhile and fight too hard to keep it if we found it. 'Course we were younger then, Jim and me. We were willing to try anything. Thought we could lick the world. But the money got away from us somehow when we went to town. We had some times, though! I remember once I got in a fight in a dance hall over a pretty little gal named Nell. She had just started working there. I was about half drunk and didn't know what I was getting into until four or five fellas jumped on me. But ol' Jim come piling in with both fists swinging, and we finally cleaned out the whole place. Of course, your pa was always good with his fists and the ladies. Then …"

Beck's smile dropped when he looked over at us. Jenny and I sat wide-eyed with surprise to hear that our father involved himself in a brawl over a dancehall girl. "I think I'll go check on the horses," Beck said and hurried away.

#

In the morning it rained, a cold misty rain. Low clouds hung over the mountains, hiding their peaks. Yet a more ominous threat loomed. Three men appeared on the hills above us to the west. One moment, they were visible on the rim of a bare ridge, then they disappeared behind the trees. They followed us like a wolf pack trailing prey.

When I mentioned them to Beck, he said, "Yeah, I been keeping an eye on them since early morning. Jenny has seen them, too."

When we stopped for a cold lunch, Beck talked about the situation. "They're probably horse thieves. Most likely picked up our trail by accident. They'll be wanting our stock, guns, money, anything they can use or sell."

"What will we do?" Jenny's eyes grew wide.

"We have to play the game for a while. They've probably noticed that Dave is a youngster, and there's a girl along. They're too cowardly to attack us in the daytime. They'll come in after dark, maybe early, maybe late. Maybe we'll just go read the law to 'em before they come calling."

"Do you have any idea who they are?" I asked.

"No, they're probably drifters and the worst kind. They just move around from town to town. They git their money from bushwhacking travelers and git their fun from murder. How I hate scum like that."

Beck's manner and the low, ominous tone of his voice made me want to walk softly and keep my distance. He had reverted to that cold, watchful manhunter I first saw above our valley. He was ready to kill again.

#

The tension tightened through the afternoon like a noose. Evening and fading light came too soon. The peaks to the east still reflected the golden glow of the setting sun while we rode in the shadowed valleys below. As the sun sunk behind the horizon, it hit me—I had not caught a glimpse of our pursuers for some time.

When asked if he thought they were gone, Beck said, "They want us to think so. We'll be making camp pretty soon. Just after dark, I'll do a little scouting around and find out for sure."

Dusk had fallen by the time supper was ready. Beck left instructions before slipping into the cover of the forest. "Jenny, a little bit after I'm gone, take your pa's rifle, pick a spot near the horses, and hide. Be quiet and don't spook them. I can tell the half-broke ones are already nervous. They may sense something or someone moving around in the woods."

"Dave, you stay here and tend the fire like nothing is wrong. I'll be back before long."

Never was the night so heavy or a fire so feeble. All sounds magnified. Time and again I jumped at noises I didn't recognize. A chaos of imagined footsteps and snapping twigs swarmed around me.

Suddenly, something huge moved from the darkness into the firelight. I was on my feet, ready to run, when I recognized Beck. He motioned for me to stay where I was and disappeared again to reemerge seconds later with Jenny.

"One of the buzzards was watching our camp all right," Beck said. "I figure he'd report back to his friends when we got settled in."

"How far away are the others?" I trembled.

"What happened to him?" Jenny said.

"He was an awful clumsy fella, walked right into a rifle butt. I also relieved him of his guns. Wouldn't want him to accidentally shoot himself while he's sleeping, you know."

"You sure are a nice, thoughtful fellow, John," I said. We all gave nervous chuckles.

"There were two more." Beck nodded back over his shoulder.

Jenny stared out into the darkness.

"I went about a quarter mile out and caught sight of a fire in a meadow."

"Now what are we going to do?" I said.

"We're gonna ride over for a friendly visit. We'll tie the horses out of sight, then Jenny and I will slip up to their camp."

"What about me?" I tingled with anticipation.

"You'll stay with our horses and keep them and the herd quiet."

The anticipation wilted like an old pumpkin vine.

Jenny ventured the most disturbing question. "Do you think there will be any killing? Maybe we can just slip out quietly and get away."

Beck looked straight at her. "There's no way we can sneak a bunch of horses out of here without leaving a trail they can follow. I don't know if there will be killing. I honestly hope not. But I know this ... If it comes to shooting, and you're not ready and willing to use that rifle, one or all of us could die tonight."

"If we just give them the horses, maybe they won't hurt us."

Beck cocked an eyebrow in her direction. "Jenny, horse stealing is a hanging offense in this country. They won't leave any witnesses."

A chill went through me.

"Is there any chance that they aren't horse thieves?" Jenny looked hopeful.

"I'll be sure and ask 'em." Beck made a small, sarcastic snort. With that, we mounted our horses and headed for the enemy camp. It was so dark I couldn't tell where I was going except by staying close behind

Jenny. Branches often brushed against me, scratching my face and arms. Finally, Beck whispered for us to stop. We dismounted, and the others handed the reins of the horses to me. Beck cautioned me to stay put and told Jenny to work her way to the left of the camp. "If we're careful," he said, "they won't hear us. If we're lucky, they'll be night blind from looking at the fire and won't be able to see anything beyond the camp. Just keep back in the shadows out of sight and be ready."

He paused, then looked back at Jenny. "If you see me go down, try to sneak back to Dave and ride for home. Leave the other horses. If the men come after you, use that rifle."

Jenny nodded.

#

Though I feared the wrath of John Beck, I wasn't going to miss the excitement. A few minutes after he and Jenny left, I tied our horses to a tree and followed. The glimmer of fire brightened the trees ahead, and I worked my way toward it.

When I reached a point where I could clearly see the whole camp without being detected, Beck was not in sight. The appearance of the two strangers held my attention. One was stocky and wore a brown, tattered jacket and a beat up Stetson. The other wore a long coat as black as his beard and the gray hat of a Confederate officer. Most obvious in his attire was the pearl-handled pistol holstered at an angle in front, visible through his open coat and readily accessible to a cross draw.

To my left, a fleeting reflection of firelight glinted on Jenny's rifle back in the trees.

Beck materialized in the circle of light, gun drawn, and commanded, "Don't make any sudden moves." Both men froze, and a tense, deadly game inched toward its awful climax.

The bearded one responded with a broad, painted grin and mock friendliness. "Well, howdy, Mister. You sure give a feller a start. Ed an' me weren't expecting no company. Were we, Ed?" The other one shook his head. "Would you like some coffee, stranger?"

"Don't reach for the coffeepot," Beck said, halting the man as he moved forward.

"You sure are a touchy one," said the bearded fellow. "Who are you, anyway?"

"Beck, John Beck."

"I bet yer one of the fellers we saw out on the trail today, drivin' some horses. You remember that, Ed?"

Ed nodded and put his coffee cup carefully beside him on the log where he sat. The bearded one took a slow step to Beck's left, putting a little more distance between himself and his partner.

"You were following us," Beck said.

"No. We just happened to be goin' the same direction. We were heading for Telluride to do some prospecting when we passed by you an' them fine lookin' horses."

"You don't have any mining tools."

"We're gonna buy some in town," said the man, smiling through his whiskers as he took another step.

"That wasn't what your friend said."

"Now who's that?"

"A tall, funny looking cuss, has a big nose and a scar over his left eye. He was snooping around our camp, but I convinced him to stay and have a long talk. And he talked a lot. He even said you boys planned to shoot us and steal our horses."

"Is he dead?" The bearded one looked real serious.

"Don't expect him for supper."

"I recall you had two others with you, looked like a boy and a girl. Where would they be now?"

"Behind you with guns aimed at your heads."

Ed looked around.

The bearded man then laughed and shook his head. "You've gone an' caught us fair. My hat's off to you, mister." The outlaw removed his hat. As he did, his right hand lunged for his pistol. Beck fired; the roar of the report shattering the night. Smoke of the explosion blurred the body of the outlaw as it sprawled backward into the darkness. Then before the other one could stand and draw, Beck whirled and leveled his pistol at the man's head.

"Try it!" Beck growled. "Try it, and I'll blow your face away."

I knew how big a .45 barrel looked six inches from a person's nose, and I felt a twinge of sympathy for Ed as he wilted before the burning glare of Beck's eyes over the top of the heavy weapon.

"Please, mister, I don't want no more trouble." The man lifted hands away from his body, all the while keeping his eyes fastened on that gun barrel.

"Your only chance to live," Beck said, "is do what I say."

"Yes, sir."

"Unfasten that gun belt with your left hand. Real careful like."

The outlaw did as told. He also turned over his rifle, knife, and a hatchet that was among his gear. He then saddled up, as instructed, and rode away, doubtlessly relieved just to be alive.

I now noticed that most of the dead man lay visible within the circle of light while his face remained hidden in the shadows. A large, dark wet spot appeared on the shirt about where his heart should have been. The corpse seemed improperly still there where life had been but a moment ago. My stomach roiled, and I was sorry I had come.

Still in my hiding place, voices came clearly to me. Beck told Jenny, "With one dead and the other two scared off, we shouldn't have any more trouble."

Jenny stepped into the light, rifle in hand. Upon looking at the dead body, she turned behind a tree and threw up.

Beck made a quick search of the camp's remnants, taking anything of value, including the dead man's weapons, horse, and rig. As they passed my place of concealment, Beck stopped and said, "Come on, Dave."

I stepped out and followed sheepishly after him. Too embarrassed to ask, I never figured out, and he never offered to tell me how he knew I was there.

As a precaution, we kept watch all that night, alternately sleeping and keeping sentry duty. I think that none of us really slept at all.

Beck didn't say another word that night. In the early, dark hours of morning he relieved me from guard duty and didn't return until breakfast. I wondered if he'd gone back to bury the dead man, but I didn't dare ask. Especially since he and Jenny remained silent until almost noon. We never mentioned the incident of the preceding night again. The question on my mind, and I think on the mind of the others, was if, or rather when, we would face violence again.

Chapter 10

THE DAY DAWNED cold, and since the last evening, the mountain peaks turned white with snow. Some of the aspen trees at the lower elevations showed color. Their leaves, fluttering vigorously in the breeze, carried the foreboding of foul weather ahead. It made me appreciate the fact that we would be spending the night in town.

We followed the San Miguel River up a narrow valley protected on both sides by high, steep slopes. Once I turned to see three black-tailed does that seemed to appear from a rock wall. They crossed behind us and disappeared into the brush along the bank near where we had just forded the icy, swift current of the river.

The town sat at the bottom of a great bowl, rimmed by rugged mountain spires. Worn, wooden buildings with false fronts lined its main dirt street. People, mostly miners, went about their business, looking only briefly at the incoming strangers leading a string of horses.

We rode through town to the place where an old livery stable sat with shabby aloofness. Before we reached it, Beck stopped short and exclaimed, "Well, I'll be!" To our right stood a dance hall with a sign out front that said *Wild Nell's*. "I'll stop in after while and see an old friend of mine," Beck said. "First, we've got business to take care of."

We went to the livery stable. The sign above the door read *Fagan's Livery-Mike Fagan, owner and dealer in fine horses*. A short, wiry old man who looked as tough as the leather harness he was mending sat on a bale of hay in front. He seemed to take little notice as Beck opened the corral gate, and we drove our horses in. Then, as we approached him, he looked up, adjusted his wire rimmed glasses, and exclaimed, "Well, John Beck, is that you?" He spit out a dark stream of tobacco juice. "I thought you was dead."

"Howdy, Mike. It's me all right, still alive and kickin'."

Fagan pushed his battered top hat back on his head. He took the rest of the wad of tobacco out of his mouth and threw it away, then wiped his fingers on his vest and shook Beck's hand. "Well, it's good to see you back in the land of the livin'. What brings you up this way?"

"I came to sell you some good horses."

"That so? Where are they?"

"Over in the corral. Can't you see?"

"I see perfect since I got my specs." Fagan wiggled his glasses.

"Take a good look then."

The old man adjusted his glasses and looked toward the corral. "Them? You call them horses? I thought they was overgrowed dogs!"

"Now, Mike, don't start that hogwash with me."

Fagan scratched his face in thought then rubbed his stubbled chin. "I couldn't git much out of those pitiful, ragged creatures. Maybe sell them to the restaurant. The cook might pass 'em off to the miners as beef."

Beck threw up his arms in exasperation. "You old crook. I thought maybe you had mellowed in your old age. But you're still the same. Do and say anything to cheat a man out of an honest dollar. Just a legalized horse thief, that's what you are."

Fagan shrugged with an innocent look on his face.

Beck chuckled. "But you're the best at it I know."

Fagan laughed. He walked over to the corral, followed by the rest of us. He put his foot up on a low rail of the fence and elbows on the top. Pulling his hat back down with a look of seriousness, he scrutinized our equine offerings. He watched and nodded. He squatted, inspecting legs and hooves. "They broke?"

"Gentle as newborn lambs," Beck replied.

Jenny and I glanced at each other. I still had bruises from breaking those *lambs*.

Fagan turned toward Beck. "Well now. After closer expert examination, I can tell that the critters have hooves instead of paws. Therefore, I will give you the benefit of the doubt." He smiled. "Come on into my office. I got a half bottle of bug juice. We'll have a drink and do some dickerin'."

In a room connected to the stable, Fagan pulled up chairs for each of us then sat behind his desk, pushing aside a pile of papers. After introductions and some reminiscing, the two men got down to earnest horse trading. It was a rousing session indeed. They wrangled and ranted between drinks. They accused each other of every kind of robbery imaginable and called each other names even the horses shouldn't have heard. At that point, Jenny walked toward the door. She nodded at me to indicate that I should follow her. I stayed where I was as she slipped out the door.

Finally, the dickering was completed, and a price agreed upon. Everyone seemed satisfied. The old friendship was still intact.

As we walked outside, we met Jenny beside the corral. Beck smiled, waved the cash at us and slipped it into his coat pocket. "We did all right, folks."

"But that was only half of what you asked for," I said.

"Yep." Our horse trading partner chuckled. "But it was a quarter more than I expected. Mike's okay. You just have to know how to speak his language."

#

Next, we headed for Nell's. A husky, fashionably dressed woman stepped out onto the walk before the dance hall. She would have looked respectable in the best sections of Denver except for the cigar that dangled from her mouth. We might have walked by her if she hadn't recognized Beck.

"Beck, honey!"

"Nellie!"

She grabbed Beck in a bear-like hug. While they squeezed each other, I looked around, hoping nobody was watching. "You rascal, where have you been keeping yourself?"

"Just moving around, Nell."

"How long has it been, five or six years?"

"It's been eleven years since I passed through here on my way back from Wyoming."

"It sure doesn't seem that long. I do remember you were in a bad way that time. I'm surprised you're still alive."

"You remember the first time I came? I was prospecting and hauling freight with a fella named Jim Foster."

"Do I! I'll never forget the night you two about tore the place down. Wildest fight I ever saw. You boys sure could raise a ruckus."

"Nellie, these are Jim Foster's kids."

"Oh?" she said, turning toward us. "I'm pleased to meet you both. Say, don't you young folks take what I said wrong. Your pa and ol' Beck here were two of the finest gents that ever walked through these doors."

She smiled back at Beck. "As a matter of fact, the night they got in the fight, it was to protect my honor. I was just a dancer then. That was a few years and several pounds ago. A big buffalo of a miner got rough with me, and John here bellered out that he wasn't gonna let nobody mistreat a lady. Then he hauled off and knocked that big varmint clear across the room. That miner had some friends, and pretty soon everybody was in on the fracas. Bottles and bodies flying everywhere. Whoo-wee! It was right down magnificent."

Wild Nell, or Big Nell, as she was now called, laughed until she shook.

Beck looked up at the building. "I see you've gone and bought the hall. Fixed it up real nice."

"Yep, about four years ago. The owner was getting on in years and decided to call it quits. Well, I'd been saving my money, and I wasn't getting any lighter on my feet, so I up and bought the place."

Nell took us in and treated us to a hot meal. Later she showed us to the hotel where Jenny and I turned in. It was hard to sleep, though, so Jenny sat with me in my room and talked before returning to her room.

My sister fell quiet for a moment before I asked, "What do you think of Nell?"

"Huh?"

"What do you think of Nellie?"

"Well, she certainly isn't the delicate flower that John remembered."

"But what do you think of *her*?"

"I guess she's all right for a dance hall lady."

"I think she's nice." I smiled. "She's sure no tart."

Jenny jerked her head toward me. "Where did you hear that word?"

"Beck."

"I might have known."

"I like her," I said.

"Fine."

"Sis, I know she runs a dance hall, but do you think she's a, you know, one of those 'ladies of the evening'?"

"I suppose you got that phrase from John, too."

"No. From Willy Johnson in school back home."

Jenny sighed and shook her head. "I don't know, but I don't think so. Papa once told Momma when they talked about coming west that men only go to the saloons for drinking, cards and talking business. There are no women allowed in there. Men dance with girls in the dance halls. Then they go to certain other 'houses' for ... Well, anyway, she's John's friend. That's all that's important."

"You're right," I said. "Maybe they're both better off for it."

"What?"

"John said if you treat a woman decent, you're both better people for it."

"Yes, I guess he has a point there."

"What do you think they are doing over there this late?"

"Dancing! Now shut up and go to sleep." Jenny jumped up and hurried off to her room.

#

I awoke the next morning to find Beck asleep in the chair next to my bed. The room was cold, and the ground below the window was powdered with a dusting of snow.

After a big breakfast and saying our goodbyes to Nell, we went to a store and bought extra supplies with the money from the sale of the horses. Jenny bought a western riding skirt and wide brimmed hat, more practical for ranching than dress and bonnet. I bought a hat somewhat like Beck's and some penny candy that I shared with the others. The rest of the money was saved for necessities unavailable in Goldstrike.

By midmorning we headed for our ranch. *Our ranch.* It had a good sound to it. The chilly weather went with us, but the day was clear, and the sun warmed the ground enough to melt the snow.

Beck halted us with a gesture. "There is a shortcut I know. It's a rugged trail that's high and narrow, but the weather looks good, and it will save us several hours. Without the other horses, we shouldn't have any problems if you two are up to it."

Jenny and I agreed.

"If we keep a good pace, we will be over the hump before any weather changes come in the late afternoon," Beck said.

We turned off the main trail and began a steep climb. It was slow going for Jenny and me. Beck glanced back at us often, as if impatient. He didn't stop us for lunch.

For a while, a rock overhang created a hollow, echoing sound from an unseen stream far below. A cliff dropped off a few feet to our left.

Just beyond the outcrop, the trail narrowed to about four feet. I could now see down a sheer drop to the stream hundreds of feet below. I took a stronger grip on the saddle horn and peered ahead at Beck. He stared at dark clouds rolling up over the sky. I turned to check on Jenny, who gazed over the edge, eyes wide.

The temperature dropped as dark, angry clouds rolled over the mountain above us, swirled down into the valley below, whipped up the side of the cliff and hit us with a mighty blast of wind.

Though the slope appeared less steep as we began to cross a rockslide area, the trail narrowed to only about two feet. The shale was unstable and, with one misstep, it could carry a horse down over a lower cliff like a waterfall of rocks.

There was no wall or trees to slow the wind, and it lashed with greater fury. Beck leaned forward to cut some wind resistance and motioned us onward. I moved Copper ahead slowly, but each new wind gust seemed to lift me up as if to fling me into the air. I looked back at Jenny. She held tight to the saddle horn with one hand and to her hat with the other as the legs of her riding skirt fluttered like flags in a gale.

To my horror, I felt Copper slide to the edge of the trail. He dug in his hooves and pushed to the side next to the mountain. But the next gust sent us back to the edge. "Lord help us, we're sure head first in the pickle barrel now." I couldn't hear my own prayer over the angry howl of the wind.

With us on top of our horses, I could tell that it created too much wind resistance. As if in agreement, Beck got down off his horse and led it. I looked back and screamed as Jenny toppled from her saddle.

I jumped off my horse in a second, crouching low against the gale as I worked my way toward her. She tried to climb back up the slippery rocks and pebbles that grew wet as the rain started in. Leaning forward, she tried to step up the slope only to slip back down several inches toward the cliff and the abyss beyond.

"Dave! Help me." Her eyes rounded with fear.

"Hang on!" I kept one foot on the trail while I dug my other foot as well as possible into the loose gravel. I reached as far as I could with my left hand, using my right hand for balance. Jenny reached and reached until she grabbed my hand. For a terrifying moment, she nearly pulled me over. I leaned back with all my might, feeling my foot slipping in the loose rocks.

Suddenly, Beck sidled up behind me, pulling on me as he handed me a rope. "Throw the end of this down to her," he yelled over the wind. I did just that, and together we pulled Jenny to safety.

#

The wind diminished as we led our horses to the end of the slide. "There's a cave up ahead where we will hole up," Beck said.

The cave was another high overhang of rock, wide and deep enough to hold us and our horses. With broken sticks gleaned from the mountain rubble, a crackling fire lighted our meager shelter. We soon warmed up and dried out as the evening shadows darkened around us.

Beck stirred the fire with a stick and moved the coffeepot to the side as we sat around, our faces a golden bronze in the flickering light.

Jenny raised her head from her cup as she said, "Thank you both for saving me today. I don't know what I would have done without my two heroes."

"You wouldn't have been in that fix if you stayed home like I told you," Beck said over his cup.

"Or if you had chosen the other route today," Jenny said, undaunted. "Anyway, all is well thanks to God's providence. He is looking after us."

Beck got up, scuffed his boot against a rock and tossed the last dregs of his coffee into the fire. "Yeah, well, I'm gonna go check the horses."

Jenny remained silent, gazing into the fire after Beck left. Finally, she turned to me. "You were very brave today."

"Aw, it wasn't nothing. You're my sister. I couldn't let you fall."

We both turned back toward the fire.

"Sis?"

"Yes?"

"You called me Dave today."

"Yeah?"

"I kinda liked it. It sounds like I'm more grown up the way Beck says it."

She smiled and nodded.

I felt kind of funny, embarrassed but good, when she hugged me.

#

By the time we reached home, autumn had exploded into the fullness of its glory. The mountain pinnacles were pure white under a clear blue sky. Groves of aspen trees glowed bright yellow and orange, looking like great bouquets amid the dark green sweep of pines. We rode into the valley, breathing deeply of the rich, fresh air and admiring the golden leaves that quaked in such a way that they seemed to glitter in the breeze.

As I headed out of the trees down into our valley, Beck said, "Hold your horse, Dave. You, too, Jenny. Let's just look for a minute before we move out into the open." It was more than two minutes as he scanned everything below us. I followed the direction of his gaze toward the cabin, the outbuildings, the whole clearing, and the edge of the forest beyond. His cautiousness always made me uncomfortable, but in the wilderness, caution was often the price for living another day.

Chapter 11

THE CABIN LOOKED sturdy and inviting. We got the horses fed and settled in the barn. Supper soon warmed in the fireplace. Fed and warm ourselves, we sat, dozing around the hearth. This was home. *Home.* Another word that had a good ring to it.

"John," Jenny said.

"Yeah?"

"Winter's coming on. Dave and I have decided that it is time you moved into Papa's room here in the house. The barn will be too cold."

Beck twisted the tip of his mustache and thought about our proposal. "Folks might talk if that gets around. You're sure you want a disreputable varmint living under your roof?"

Jenny laughed. "Yes."

"Yep." I agreed with her.

"We know that we will be safe with you in here," Jenny said.

Beck said nothing for a moment. His eyes seemed kind of sad as he turned toward the fireplace. "Safe ..." He stared somewhere far off beyond the flames.

#

It felt odd to hear John Beck stirring below my loft, moving his few belongings into my father's room. Odd, but comforting. I once said that I suspected that John Beck was dangerous, but not to us. That was proving to be true.

#

Beck seemed a little awkward, almost embarrassed, entering from Pa's room the next morning. "I can't believe I overslept. It must be near six o'clock." He scratched the stubble on his chin. "Something sure smells good out here, though."

"Fresh coffee, biscuits, and the last of the bacon," Jenny said from the fireplace.

"Tomorrow, we'll ride into Goldstrike and buy supplies from Joe Warner." Beck settled himself at the table. "We should have enough money left from the horse sale to buy a few cattle later. The mares we kept back will foal in the spring, and we'll have us a real working ranch."

Jenny and I smiled at each other.

As we sat to breakfast, Beck reached for our hands before Jenny began to pray.

#

As we prepared to leave for a hunting trip, Beck gave instructions to Jenny. "Don't take any long walks or rides and get yourself lost. Stay close to the cabin. If any strangers come by, don't talk to them. Just tell them to water their horses and move on. And whatever you do, don't let them in. I'm leaving the shotgun. Keep it handy, and, if you have to, use it."

"Stop worrying. I can take care of myself. And I never get lost in the woods. Furthermore, Papa taught me how to use firearms. I'm a pretty fair shot if I do say so myself. I can handle outlaws, hostile Indians, or herds of stampeding buffaloes. Now please get going, so we can have meat for supper."

#

In the forest, high above our valley, Beck watched everywhere with those sharp eyes. He drew in the reins of his horse. I moved Copper up beside him as he pulled a pair of army binoculars from his saddlebag and scanned a far ridge. "Look over there." He handed them to me.

I adjusted the binoculars and looked along the ridge to a gap in the trees. There, moving across the opening, was a large animal. "A bear."

"A grizzly bear, the biggest, meanest, most cantankerous critter on Earth."

"Will it come after us?"

"No. He's already caught our scent and is starting to move off."

"How do you know when one's out to get you?"

"Like most animals, a bear will leave you alone if you give it plenty of room. But if you come up on it sudden or get between a female and her cub, you're in real trouble. Sometimes, if you stand still, hold your ground, and talk to it, it will recognize you as a human and back off. At least that's what the Indians say. It may even take a false run at you, just to scare you off, and then walk away. But if it's looking you right in the eye with the hair bristling up on its back, chopping its jaws and slobbering, you're in deep manure. Then you better shoot it or get up a tree. Otherwise, you're gonna be meat."

We moved on with me looking over my shoulder. Soon Beck showed me deer tracks, rubs on trees, and flat spots in the grass where deer had rested. Then, following a fresh set of tracks, he motioned for me to stop and dismount. I crept behind him to a cluster of rocks. "Stay low and quiet," he whispered.

I peeked over his shoulder as he aimed his rifle. A mule deer headed into an aspen grove beyond a small clearing. At the same moment, Beck's rifle discharged, nearly bursting my eardrums.

The animal was fat and healthy in its gray-brown autumn coat. "Get my rope and help me haul this thing up to that branch over there."

With the deer secured to the tree, Beck turned to me. "Have you ever field-dressed a deer?"

"No. Pa always did that."

Beck handed me his knife. "Well, here you go."

I hesitated.

"Remember what I said a hundred times. 'To be a rancher, you have to learn …'"

"To do the things that are hard." I repeated the now familiar sentence.

Beck guided me as I cut into the hide, squinting my eyes and wrinkling my nose as I dropped the steaming entrails to the ground.

With the deer carcass secured on the pack mule, we rode across a clearing from which we could see our valley far below. A man rode away from the cabin.

Beck dropped the rope to the packhorse. "Bring the deer in," he said over his shoulder.

"Hyah!" Beck spurred his mount into a gallop and raced toward the ranch. I rode hard as I could while hanging onto the lead rope, trying to catch up to him. My heart beat like the horse's hooves within my chest.

In front of the cabin, Beck leaped from his horse and ran inside.

"Jenny! Jenny where are you?" he called as I reached the porch.

Jenny came down the stairs with a broom in her hand. "I'm right here. Is something wrong?"

"Who was that man who rode out of here just now? What did he want?" Agitation strained Beck's voice.

"His name is Luke Dawson. He's very nice. A little while ago, I heard someone call from outside. I opened the door, and there was a big, young cowhand on the finest black horse I've ever seen." Her cheeks reddened slightly. "He said he was riding the grub line, looking for a job. Of course, I told him we couldn't afford an extra hand, but he might find somebody looking for men in town. I was a little afraid at first, but the more we talked, I could tell that he was a gentleman. He looked hungry, too, so I fixed him a breakfast of biscuits and coffee before he left."

During Jenny's story, a dark expression came over Beck's face. When she mentioned the breakfast, he exploded. "You mean you let him in the house?"

"I just fixed him something to eat, and ..."

"Didn't I tell you not to let anybody in?"

"Yes, but it was all right. Nothing happened. I don't understand why you're getting so upset. Besides, I ..."

"It was a stupid thing to do!" Beck cursed.

"I told you I wouldn't have that kind of language in my house!" Jenny yelled back.

"Don't you know you could've been hurt or killed or ... Or taken advantage of?" Beck paused a second. "Or maybe that thought crossed your mind."

Jenny's eyes flamed, and she slapped Beck's face so hard it sounded like a shot.

A deathly silence followed as my sister and I froze with horror at what she had done. And its possible result.

I waited without breathing, expecting to see murder committed. Beck turned his red face back to Jenny. His eyes smoldered with the same look I'd seen when he aimed his gun at the face of the outlaw in the forest. Surely, no living person had ever touched John Beck in such a manner without facing a terrible retaliation.

Something awful appeared to struggle within Beck, trying to find release in his clenched fists. Gradually it faded, and he let his breath out slowly. He said nothing but left the cabin. Only then did we begin to breathe again. Jenny hurried through the door to her room, tears in her eyes.

#

We talked after Jenny finally came out of her room. Her eyes were still red. "I don't understand that man," I said. "Why'd he blow up so? Jenny, maybe you shouldn't have trusted a stranger too much, but it turned out all right. It's almost like there's more bothering him than just what you said."

"We don't really know much about him." Jenny wiped her eyes on a handkerchief. "Like a wild animal that seems calm at first but can't really be tamed."

"He's a strange man ... and a dangerous one. The question is, is he going to be dangerous to us?"

#

It was a nearly silent supper that night. The tension fell so thick that a Bowie knife could hardly cut through it. All I remember is somebody saying something about passing the potatoes.

Beck sat silently, looking humble, a state seldom seen in him. But Jenny stayed quiet only until it came time to wash the dishes. Tin plates, pots, and pans banged and rattled as if she tried to beat the dirt out.

Beck went outside, mumbling something about chores. I hurried to help dry the dishes, then escaped to the outhouse. As I returned, the back door opened, and Jenny stepped into the light with the pan of dishwater. Just as she threw out the water and turned to go back in, Beck stepped into the light of the doorway.

"Jenny." His voice was low and husky.

She froze in position but did not turn around.

"Jenny, I'm sorry about what I said. Real sorry. It was mean. You are a real lady and don't deserve such disrespect."

"You're right. I don't." She still did not turn around.

"I know you would never do anything improper. But there's people out there ... well, men, that is. Men that would do something bad to a woman by herself. What I mean to say is ... I worry about you when you're all alone."

Beck cleared his throat. "Several years back I left ..." He shook his head. "Anyway, I'm real concerned about your safety. When I thought you might've been in danger, I ... I just kinda blew up when I shouldn't have. I'm sorry."

Jenny gave a sigh and turned around to face Beck. "I am grateful for your concern. I guess you are a gentleman in your own way. I should appreciate a person who wants to protect my honor. I accept your apology."

"Thank you."

"Good night." Jenny stepped past Beck on her way into the cabin then looked back over her shoulder. "By the way, you didn't give me time to explain it before, but I didn't let the young man into the house. I served him breakfast on the porch."

Beck nodded, then stepped out into the dark as Jenny entered the cabin. On his way across the barn lot, he stopped and pulled down a harness from the fence that he had mentioned needed repairing. Then, he stopped and looked up at the stars for a long time.

#

Trouble appeared again in the form of Frank Maxwell and two of his hired hands. They rode in about midmorning. Maxwell was in the lead on a fine roan gelding. With him was a man he introduced as his foreman, Bill Oaks, and Jud Sykes, thin and mean-looking as ever.

Jenny and I stood before the cabin and watched them ride up. Beck had disappeared somewhere out back.

"Morning, folks." Maxwell said with his oily grin. "You youngsters sure have done a nice job with this place. Yes, sir, a lot better than I would've expected."

"We like it," I said.

"I sure was sorry to hear about what happened to your pa. I would've come sooner, but I've been away for a while, taking care of some business."

"I take it that you've got business here now," Jenny said.

Maxwell leaned forward in his saddle. "Well, yes, I do, as a matter of fact. Your pa and I had a real good talk about this place the last time we met in town. He thought it might be a mistake to try to make it through the winter here. We have real bad winters, you know. He said he might consider selling in the fall, and I made him a real good offer. Now, if we can go inside, I can …"

Jenny and I glanced at each other. "We're not selling," she said.

"What?"

"We're not selling."

"But I'm offering cash. Four thousand dollars."

"Our pa didn't offer our home to anybody," I said. "The only way he'd give up is by being shot in the back by a coward."

"What do you mean by that, boy?" Maxwell asked, a mean sneer on his face.

I folded my arms across my chest. "You can't do business here, Mr. Maxwell, so you better leave."

"You talk big for a wet-behind-the-ears kid. You'll both be dead in the snow before spring."

"I doubt that." John Beck spoke from the doorway of the cabin.

"Who are you?" Maxwell demanded, turning.

Beck's right hand hung close to his holster. "Just the hired man."

Bill Oaks leaned over to Maxwell and whispered, "That's John Beck."

Frank stiffened at the name. "Are these youngsters staying on your advice?"

"Nope. My boss, Mr. Foster here," Beck nodded toward me, "says we're staying, so I reckon we are."

"If you know what's good for you and these children, you'll talk some sense into them and have them take my offer. It's a good deal." Irritation grew in Frank Maxwell's voice. He appeared uncertain now that he was dealing with a man and two healthy, stubborn youths rather than the confused, starving orphans he probably expected to find.

"I think you better leave now," I said.

Maxwell hesitated.

"Mr. Foster asked you to leave twice now." Beck's voice was firm and cold. "I suggest you do it. And as for your money, you can …" He glanced over at Jenny and never finished the sentence. But he continued, "Well, you know what you can do with it. I figure you've heard it before."

"You're making a bad mistake, a real bad mistake." Maxwell's voice tensed.

All during the conversation, Jud Sykes had been silent, but his eyes never left Jenny. He looked her over from head to foot with the carnivorous look of a vulture admiring a piece of raw meat. He smiled slightly, but it wasn't a kind smile. Jenny never appeared to notice him. But it made me angry inside just to watch his face.

As Maxwell and Oaks turned to ride away, Sykes moved his horse closer to Jenny and tipped his hat. His grin widened, and he winked at me as if sharing some kind of crude joke. He hurried to catch his companions.

"That Frank Maxwell sure is persistent," I said.

"He'll be back," Beck said. "He's going to be trouble because that is one hungry man."

"He's not the only one." Jenny shuddered.

Chapter 12

THE WORLD WAS blue in the predawn glow that seems to rise from the earth to soften the heavy black shadows of night. As we saddled our horses in that hushed and dreamlike hour, one could believe that time had paused and the sun would be a long time in coming. But the animals knew. Birds tentatively began to sing, and a fox padded silently across the clearing toward its den.

Beck was taking me on another hunting trip to add more meat to our winter stores. The horses whinnied softly with nervous expectation at our unusually early activity. They couldn't be more nervous or excited than me. This was my first trip far into the backcountry to search out the large, majestic elk.

From a mountain ridge, the earth appeared to roll away in waves of pine forests into the misty distance. Our party of two riders and two pack mules wound its way through the high country. The sun had just set a high mountain ridge aflame with its scarlet radiance when a wild, mysterious sound floated up from the valley. In the cold air it was like a distant bugle, rising into a high-pitched whistle. Never had I heard such a haunting sound.

"What's that?" I turned to my hunting companion, wide-eyed.

"That is the challenge call of a bull elk. During the rutting season, a bull will gather a herd of cows and bellow like that to dare all the other bulls around to try and take them away. Like as not, another male will come along and they'll fight it out until one has enough and runs off. You can hear 'em carrying on a mile away."

Before long, more bugling radiated through the forest. One seemed far and one close. Soon, the clatter of striking antlers reverberated from the valley below.

"They sound close," I said in a whisper.

"They're still a quarter mile away," Beck said. "Sound carries up here."

"Will we see a lot of them?" I asked.

"Maybe. They've been moving down from higher up the mountain as the weather turns colder. Keep an eye open for signs like scraped bark on trees and big flattened-out places in the grass. The rutting season's about over now, and they'll be going on down into the sheltered valleys. Those we heard fighting are probably a couple stubborn ol' boys that haven't given up yet.".

We came to a stream, and Beck got down to look at the frosted ground. "Elk's been here. See these tracks, bigger than a deer's, and that tore up ground along the bank? The tracks are sharp and fresh, a few hours old. They've been moving at a slow walk back up from the water."

We moved cautiously across the stream and through a clump of yellow, quaking aspens to the edge of a large clearing. On the far side of the meadow, a herd of cows grazed. Near them, the bull admired his hard-won harem. He was a fine sight, standing almost five feet at the shoulder, and weighing maybe seven hundred pounds. His antlers grew from his head like a long, royal crown, stretching over his back beyond his heavy shoulders.

A sudden breeze sent a shower of leaves fluttering down around us, and the elk became alert. "The wind is shifting," Beck whispered. "We'll have to work our way around and try to come in closer on the other side."

We rode in a wide arc through the forest. We had been traveling for perhaps half an hour when Beck reined his horse to a halt. He was cautious and watchful as he drew his rifle from its saddle scabbard.

To our right, a shallow depression in the ground containing the partially eaten carcass of an elk, scantily covered with dirt and leaves. "That's a grizzly kill," he said. "Not too many of them out this late in the season. Maybe that same one we saw the other day. But they're nothing to fool with. Bad tempers, and they don't take to anybody disturbing their food caches."

"Are they real dangerous?" I asked.

"A big one can break a horse's neck with one swat of his paw. They got teeth like railroad spikes and claws like Bowie knives. Does that answer your question?"

"Whoo-wee!"

"Keep your eyes open. We came for elk, not bear." We moved more cautiously after that. I, for one, wanted to get a better look at a real grizzly bear—just as long as it wasn't too close.

I almost forgot the bear and the hunt as I rode on and contemplated the movements of an eagle floating in lazy arcs on the air currents high above, peaceful and free, unconcerned with the earth below. It was framed there by the clear blue sky and gray mountain walls, nearly touching thin white clouds.

Hunger pulled me from my dreaming, and I was about to ask Beck if we could eat when he stopped us again. On a flat area near a canyon I caught a glimpse of an elk disappearing into some brush.

"Tie the horses here and we'll work closer on foot. Stay low behind me and be quiet," Beck whispered. With much effort we worked our way through the brush. Once I stumbled, snapping a twig, and Beck shot a warning glance at me. I felt like a real dunce. I proceeded with the utmost care so I wouldn't repeat the incident.

It seemed like we took forever to find our prey. Beck didn't lead me to where we saw the elk but where he expected it to appear next. Finally, he motioned for me to stop. There we waited, watching an opening in the bushes. Eventually we caught sight of something ahead of us moving to the left.

"It's farther out than I figured on, can't git a good shot here. We'll have to move again," Beck whispered.

Just then, a second movement rustled the brush. "There's two of them," Beck whispered. "We'll take the closer one. We only need one. Besides, you'll only git a chance at one shot."

"Me?"

"Yep. This is going to be your shot."

Remembering my fiasco with the moose, my heart raced.

We moved on again until Beck halted in a place where the foliage wasn't quite so thick. Once more, we waited. With a nod, Beck directed my glance ahead. An elk moved into an opening in the bushes. The animal stood broadside to us, presenting a perfect shot, less than a hundred yards away. Excitement shot through me until I thought I would burst.

Beck looked at me, his movement barely perceptible. This was the moment.

My father's Winchester weighed heavy as I slowly raised it and aimed. I hesitated, my heart beating a fast *rat-a-tat* against my chest. The front sight of my weapon wavered all over the body of the elk from my shaking hands. I sensed Beck's questioning look. I feared disappointing him most of all.

Then, John Beck's often repeated instructions returned to my mind as clearly as if he spoke aloud at that moment. 'When you aim to kill, forget fear and doubt and everything else in the world. Just take a deep breath and let it out slow. Focus on nothing but that bead on the target. Then squeeze the trigger. Don't pull because it will become a jerk. Focus and squeeze ... squeeze ... squeeze ...' The rifle roared and thudded hard against my shoulder. The elk jumped then ran into the bushes.

I felt sick with disappointment until Beck yelled. "You hit it! Looked like a heart shot. He'll run a ways but not far. Get the horses and we'll go find it."

We mounted our horses and galloped after the mortally wounded animal. We tore through brush and ducked under branches. Suddenly, a loud moan sounded behind a cluster of bushes on the left. The horses went wild, neighing and dancing in circles as a huge grizzly rose, head and shoulders above the tall bushes.

"Keep your horse steady," Beck ordered as he drew his rifle. "He hasn't decided whether to walk away or charge. So, just move back the way we came."

The frantic horses would not be controlled. Mine reared and bucked. The bear gave out a horrendous roar like nothing else I've heard on this earth. Then, he dropped out of sight. Only the crash and swaying of the bushes indicated the monster's approach.

"It's coming!" Beck yelled. "Get out of here." He could have saved his breath because my own mount seemed to be running four ways at once. With a quick jump, he left me on the ground and ran for home.

So began a nightmare that can still wake me from a sound sleep. Beck jumped from his horse and stood between me and the oncoming bear. He yelled at me to run, but I couldn't move. The charge of the beast, the shaking of the bushes, and roaring had the impact of a hurricane, forcing me to the ground in the midst of my terror.

I hardly understood how Beck could stand so steadily before such a force. But he stood, immovable as a boulder with his rifle aimed at the point where the bear would appear in another second. The bushes parted as the grizzly tore into the open with all the fury of a runaway freight train. Its face was twisted in rage and filled with teeth. The bristled fur shook with the jolting power of its mad run.

Beck fired without visible effect. He levered another bullet and fired again. The furious animal came on. Beck cursed, and the gun roared again with the bear only feet away, closing fast. Then the grizzly heaved up on hind legs, towering over Beck, to lunge upon the man.

With the fourth shot, the beast fell at Beck's feet.

Nothing moved. No one breathed for a long time. Not the bear, not Beck, and not me. Finally, Beck let his breath out slowly in a long sigh. He then prodded the bear with the rifle barrel to make sure the animal was dead. It remained still.

"You all right?" Beck asked.

I nodded, still unable to speak. Only then did I realize that I stood with a large rock in my hand. I didn't remember moving or picking it up.

Beck looked at me. "What were you planning to do with that?"

"I guess I was going to bean that bear in the head with it if it got you down."

"You know that grizzly would have had you for dessert."

"Probably so. But I figure I would have at least given him a headache to remember me by."

Beck gave one of his rare grins and chuckled. "You sure are getting some sand to you. You'll be a man worthy to ride the river with."

I breathed easier again.

"Sure was a big rascal," he said, looking back at the grizzly. "It'll run six hundred pounds, maybe more."

My legs wobbled as I approached the body. The whole incident happened so fast that the silent heap on the ground seemed unrelated to the great beast that rose up above the bushes just moments ago.

I bubbled with excitement and praise. "You sure were something, John! I mean that was the greatest thing I ever saw, standing there face-to-face with a grizzly and not budging. You're the bravest man I know—except Pa, of course."

"Of course." He smiled again.

"That bear sure was determined to git rid of us. Let's see what he was protecting," Beck said. I followed him through the bushes to the spot where we first saw the grizzly, guns still at the ready. There on the ground was our elk.

"Well, we better git after our horses." Beck pushed back his hat and wiped his forehead with his arm. "We got a lot of work ahead of us."

It took us another hour to find the horses. During the whole time, I talked about our adventure with the bear.

"Well, you had your part in this exploit, Mr. Foster. You made a great shot today. We have enough meat to carry us far into winter because of you."

My chest swelled.

#

Upon returning to the sight of the kill, I helped Beck cut up the elk and pack the meat on a mule, saving also the hide and antlers. Next, he skinned the grizzly for its warm coat. It was with great reluctance that the other pack mule finally allowed the hated bear skin to be placed on top of its pack.

When we reached home, I rushed in the door to be the first to tell Jenny about our experience. She listened with horror to the story and declared that a youngster like me shouldn't be taken on such dangerous excursions into the wilderness. Beck and I just looked at each other and grinned.

After the conversation dwindled, Jenny turned to Beck and said softly, "That was a very brave and noble thing you did in protecting my brother. Thank you."

"Sometimes bravery is just knowing that you can't run faster than your enemy," he said with a hint of a smile.

Chapter 13

THE DAY AFTER we'd prepared and stored the meat and hides, we went to town to buy those goods that couldn't be obtained from the forest. The morning was gray and chilly with the promise of snow in the heavy clouds. The aspens were stark and bare against the dark green pines.

Two hours after we started, the wagon creaked up to Warner's general store in Goldstrike. The town consisted of one store, one saloon, and a blacksmith shop.

The simple, wooden buildings needed a fresh coat of paint. Three log cabins sheltered the town's half dozen inhabitants. Several other cabins remained abandoned by the miners who had failed to find any useful metal in the holes that dotted the hillsides.

Joe Warner's store was a warm, friendly place. A potbellied stove relieved customers of winter's chill. Shelves lined the walls, holding a variety of goods from pots and pans to work shirts and a small pile of dress material. The glass case on the main countertop held an array of small items including jackknives, hard candy, and tobacco.

Joe greeted us from behind the counter. "Howdy, folks. What can I do for you today?"

"Mr. Warner, this Is John Beck," I said. "He's our ... our business partner."

Joe hesitated a second as he looked at John, then offered his hand. "Beck."

Beck shook his hand then handed the storekeeper a paper. "We got us a list of things we'll be needing for winter."

"Comin' right up. You all feel free to look around for anything else that strikes your fancy while I get these things."

Joe placed flour, coffee, bacon, and other essentials on the counter. We moved about the store, looking at things that appealed to our interest if not our wallets. Beck pointed out some heavy sheepskin coats that he said would be almost as good as buffalo hides for keeping us warm in the cold days ahead.

I noticed Jenny talking to a young man by the door and tapped Beck on the shoulder. "You remember when you said we'd have to watch out for Jenny? Well, I think spring might come early this year."

That was the first time I heard Beck really laugh.

"You folks have a good winter," Joe said as we left. "Nice meeting you, Beck." John nodded back and hoisted the last box of supplies to his shoulder. With everything loaded and ready to go, Beck hesitated, looking toward the saloon. He untied his horse from the back of the wagon. "You two go on. I think I'll stay awhile and take care of some more business."

Jenny shot a disapproving look at him, but she nodded to me, and, as I flicked the reins, the wagon rattled toward home.

We prepared supper and ate. Night fell, but Beck did not return from town. The old clock on the mantel struck twelve o'clock when Jenny went to bed.

I was still awake an hour later when startled by a terrible commotion outside. I grabbed a lantern and threw open the door. Jenny came running out, still in her nightgown.

Beck galloped his horse into the yard, whooping like an Indian, waving his pistol in one hand and a bottle in the other. He holstered the gun and reined the lathered horse to an abrupt halt. He tried to jump off dramatically, but he missed the ground with his feet and landed flat on his back.

He remained so still that, for a moment, we thought he might be dead. Then he raised himself to a sitting position and looked at us through bleary eyes. "Whatcha' starin' at?" he mumbled. "I just misshed m' footin' a li'l bit."

"You're drunk." Jenny folded her arms in disgust.

"Well, a man's gotta cut loose sometimes an' make a noise in the world, or nobody'll know he's alive," Beck sputtered.

"We better get him inside before he freezes in that position," I said.

We attempted to hoist Beck's two hundred sodden pounds off the ground. I pushed while Jenny pulled, finally getting him up on his knees.

As he lurched to his feet, Beck put his arm around Jenny's waist.

He then stopped and looked at her. "Why, you ain't got much on, girl! I always told Maria to be careful about the night air. Always dress warm. A cold, damp wind will kill y' as sure as yer born."

He then stared at the ground and groaned. "Oh, Maria, Maria … I'm sorry!"

We nudged him toward the door, but he stopped again. "I have heard the owl hoot, and I've seen the elephant!" He gave a belch that ended with a hiccup. "I feel like the elephant sat on me. That bug juice an' Mexican food do awful things to a man's gut." With that, he staggered over to the corner of the cabin and vomited.

Afterward, he seemed a little more alert and allowed Jenny, who had donned a robe, to guide him into the house. We tumbled him into the bed in our father's room. I took Beck's horse to the barn to rub it down and feed it. He was in no condition to do it.

When I returned to the cabin, Jenny still paced before the fireplace in a fury. "That is the most exasperating man I ever met! He's a trial to my Christian patience. Every time I think there is something worth saving in him, he does something to destroy my illusion. One minute he does something brave and noble, and the next he is the most disgusting, broken down, drunken mess I've ever seen."

"Take it easy, Sis. He hasn't been drunk before. Maybe he won't do it again. Anyway, I'll talk to him about it in the morning."

"I'll give him a talking-to he won't forget." Jenny stomped her foot.

"You're not going to tell him to leave, are you?"

"No." She sighed. "Not yet. Not unless worse problems come up. You were right. We still need him through the winter. At least the weather should keep him away from town and the saloon for a while."

"Well, Beck said that whiskey is good for snake bite." It was the wrong thing to say in front of my temperance-minded sister.

"I declare! You're getting to be more like him every day."

"Who do you think Maria is?" I said, trying to change the subject.

"I have no idea. His past is extremely mysterious and no doubt very questionable."

That was a point for which I couldn't find an argument.

#

When I awoke, a thin dusting of white crystals lay on the windowsill inside the loft. I opened the window and shutters to discover the world had been transformed by two feet of sparkling snow. It even frosted the trees. As I brushed some pine branches next to the cabin, they exploded with puffs of cold, crystalline powder.

I rushed to breakfast, anxious to get out in the snow, but in the main room, an atmosphere of cold solemnity proved more sobering than that outside. Jenny prepared breakfast as I added wood to the fire. Beck stared into his coffee cup and looked like someone recovering from a long illness. No one spoke, so I sat at the table and suffered the heavy silence.

Jenny set plates of bacon and eggs and a warm loaf of bread before us. After everyone sat, she said a short prayer. During that prayer I kept my eyes cracked open to watch the other two diners. "Lord, we thank Thee for this bounty and Your many blessings ... Including Your forgiveness for the sins of those who are willing to ask." She glanced at Beck and then closed her eyes again. "Amen."

The silence continued. Finally, Beck shoved his chair back from the table and stood. "I've seen livelier folks in graveyards. I reckon 'cause I got drunk last night that shocks you down to your little Sunday-go-to-meeting hearts. Well, the fact is, children, there are people in the world who drink and sometimes git drunk, and do a whole lot of other things that you wouldn't call nice. That's the way the world is, and you gotta live here 'cause there ain't no place else. You live the way you want and leave everybody else to their own business."

"We are aware that your life is your own business," Jenny said, her voice tense, her eyes focused on the table. "I'm sure that you can also understand that what happens in our house is our business."

"I didn't ask for this job," Beck spoke in a more subdued tone. "I promised I'd help you get started and get you through the winter. Come spring I'll be gone, and your home will be all yours again. That is unless you want me to leave now. Go or stay, it's the same to me."

"No!" I blurted out. Then I looked at my sister to see what the effect would be.

"Let's not let this thing get out of hand." Jenny folded her napkin twice. "We don't have any complaints about what you've done for us. You've been honest and done a good job. I don't think we could have made it this far without you. It's just that if the drinking is a problem of yours, it could become a problem of ours."

"You don't have to worry about that." Beck shook his head.

"Then we want you to stay." As I said it, I looked at Jenny for confirmation. She slowly nodded agreement.

Beck went to the door and took his new sheepskin coat from the wall. As he put it on, he turned back toward us. "Jenny, I'm sorry that I disappointed you again. It was a fool thing to do. Just don't set your measure of any man too high. All men make mistakes sometimes, even the best of them, like your pa. If you judge all people by holy perfection, you'll always be disappointed, and you'll do a wrong to the person you're judging. Look for the good you can find and start your measure there."

He turned away, but stopped, running his hand through his hair. "Oh, by the way, something did come out of that fandango last night. Men talk more when they've got a little tonsil paint in 'em, and a couple good ol' boys at the saloon told me some interesting things about our neighbor Maxwell. The word is he's a real bad case. He comes from somewhere back east where they say he was involved in a killing. He disappeared for a while and then showed up in Texas with a lot of money." He turned a little, halfway facing the room again. "Since he came here, he's bought out or run out two different ranchers. They each had spreads near his. Also, he's been moving in a lot of cattle from somewhere down south. Nobody knows from just where, though. Now, the hands that work for him are a bad bunch, too. There's a few regular cowpunchers. The rest are small time thieves and gunmen."

"I'll bet we're next on Maxwell's run-out list," I said.

"I wouldn't be surprised. We'll keep a close eye on him and see what happens." Beck then stepped through the door but paused halfway out and said, more to himself than to us, "I wonder if there's a reward poster out on Maxwell."

Chapter 14

As JOHN BECK predicted, the winter was cold and snowy. We soon fell into a routine of toting wood, feeding stock, and trying to keep warm.

As if to break the monotony, a restless roan mare named Serenity found ways to get out of the corral or barn and wander off into the woods a couple times. When we found her, she'd follow us back home as easily as if going to a tea. Once inside the corral, she became fidgety and unpredictable except that she could be counted on to keep one eye on the forest beyond the creek.

Winter escalated, and the snows fell with more intensity. Great billows covered the earth and reached for the lower edges of the cabin roof. The creek cut an icy black course between its rounded alabaster banks.

At times, there would be a short thawing, or great, cold winds would rage down the valley and blast away much of the snow. Then, the storms would return with stronger determination, and we would have to use snowshoes to get to the barn.

The approach of Christmas offered a point of brightness in the grim bleakness of winter. Jenny was aglow with seasonal cheer. She was a child. She was Saint Nicholas. She was a whirlwind of preparations. "I'm not going to allow weather, hard times, or anything else to stand above the glory of Christmas," she declared.

Her enthusiasm affected us both, though Beck not nearly as much as me. The morning of Christmas Eve Jenny announced, "John, we need a tree, and you are elected to cut it."

"A tree?" He groaned.

"Yes, a Christmas tree. It can be your contribution to this great occasion."

"Open the door."

"What?"

"Open the door and look outside and tell me what you see."

Jenny opened the door and peered out into the chilled morning air. "I see snow, mountains, the creek, and the forest."

"There are ten million trees out there." Beck waved his arm. "Anytime you want to see a tree, just open up the door and look all you like."

"Now, don't be a grouch. The cold air will lift your spirits." Jenny thrust Beck's coat at him.

"You might as well go," I said. "She's got her mind set."

"Oh, all right. I'll get you the biggest tree in the whole woods. You can stick it clear through the roof. Will that make you happy?"

"Perfectly." She laughed.

"Christmas is for children, you know. For children and crazy young women," Beck said with a snort as he stomped out the door.

I yanked on my coat and boots to follow Beck. After saddling the horses, we rode through a rolling sea of snow. The only sounds were the soft purring of the pine trees at the caress of the wind and the hiss of the sled tied to a long rope behind Beck's horse.

We stopped in a grove of young spruce saplings. "Well, we ought to find something here." Beck dismounted and drew the ax from the sled. In a few seconds, he pointed to one that caught his interest. "What do you think of that one, Dave?" He indicated a bushy young tree about seven feet tall.

"It looks fine to me."

"Now, Jenny would probably prefer one like that." He grinned as he aimed his ax toward a long, straight lodge pole pine about twenty feet high.

"If that's not what she wants, you can bet she'll send us out again." We chuckled.

"Your sister sure gets excited about this Christmas business."

"Yeah, we both do, I guess. I get anxious sometimes thinking about the present I might get."

"Present?"

"Sure, didn't you ever wonder what you were getting for Christmas?"

"I don't remember." Beck took a couple firm swings at the tree. "When I was just a nubbin, getting food on the table was a celebration in itself." He swung the ax in the long, easy strokes of an experienced woodsman. The whack of the ax rang through the forest. The man's heavy breathing created clouds of mist in the frosty air. When the chopping ceased, his mustache was white with frozen moisture.

By the time we packed the tree on the sled, the afternoon had waned. It was dusk when we looked down from the ridge at the cabin. How peaceful it appeared there, nestled on the blue-tinted snow beneath the fading alpenglow on the mountains. A rising moon hung in silver radiance in the blue-black sky, spangled with winking stars. Never had the warm yellow light from the cabin windows looked so inviting.

Jenny was delighted with the tree. She put me to setting it up while Beck warmed himself by the fire and she finished the supper. The preparation of the meal had taken all day and filled the room with a tempting fragrance. We gave satisfied sighs and compliments about the roast duck with special sauce, vegetables canned from Jenny's garden, and fresh bread, hot from the oven. Jenny glowed with pride and appreciation at our praises.

Near the end of the meal, Jenny slipped into her room and returned with a cake glowing with candles.

Beck's eyes widened. "What's this?"

Jenny laughed. "It's a birthday cake."

"Yeah, but who's having a birthday?"

"Most everybody in this room," I said.

"You see," Jenny said as she placed the cake on the table, "first, Christmas celebrates Jesus' birthday. Then Dave just turned thirteen two days ago, and I was born on December twenty-ninth. Therefore, we celebrate all our birthdays on Christmas."

"That's right handy." After a quick count, Beck pointed to the candles. "Looks like there's thirty-two."

Jenny nodded to the cake. "That's thirteen for Dave and nineteen for me. We don't know your age. If we put on all the candles for Jesus' birthday, we'd need a cake bigger than the room."

I grinned. "That would be all right with me."

The three of us blew out the tiny flames. Jenny paused as she cut the cake. "When is your birthday, John?"

"I don't rightly recall. Sometime in '49, I think. My folks were poor and thought more about surviving than celebrating."

Jenny gave him a kind of sad look, then brightened. "Well, we'll just count this as your birthday, too. Happy Birthday, John."

"Thanks. Now, let's eat this fine-looking cake."

#

After supper we decorated the tree with red berries and colored paper bows. Ah, but it was a soul-warming sight in quiet splendor there in the corner!

Beck seemed content, having placed himself in the rocking chair by the fireplace. He looked at the pretty tree. He listened to the carols we sang and the Christmas story Jenny read from our old family Bible. He watched with mild amusement as Jenny and I exchanged gifts, a scarf and mittens knitted by my sister and a wooden spice rack I had carved for her.

Beck rose from the table and stretched. "That was real nice, kids. The food great, too. My compliments to the cook." He nodded to my sister.

Jenny and I exchanged glances. I started to reach behind the Christmas tree, but she held up one finger to signal me to wait a moment.

John had moved over by the mantel and, for several minutes, stared at the wooden nativity set we'd brought from Indiana. It nestled among fresh pine boughs. Each piece—manger, people, even a camel—had been intricately carved by our father.

"His was the greatest gift of all," said Jenny, her voice soft over Beck's shoulder. "Jesus gave his life for all of us. When we confess our sins and ask Him into our hearts, He forgives us and gives us eternal life."

Beck looked at Jenny, then at the miniature wooden figure in the manger. "There's only two people in the world I'd lay down my life for. They're both dead." He walked to the stove, poured a cup of coffee, and sat back in the chair.

Jenny gave a sigh, touched the manger, and turned to me. I nodded to her. "There is one thing left to do, John."

"What?"

"Pass out your presents," She handed him a package.

Beck looked genuinely surprised and unsure as to what he should do.

"Well, open it," I said.

He pulled the brown paper apart and held up a woolen muffler Jenny had knitted. "Looks warm," he said.

"There's another." I held out an old, finely made pocketknife. "It was Pa's. You're his friend and, well, we thought he would like for you to have it."

"Being your pa's, you should keep this."

"Pa gave me my own when I was ten."

Beck looked at the knife with admiration. He then looked at us as if at a loss for words. Nodding, he said, "It's a good knife ... a nice muff. Thanks ... I'm sorry. I didn't think to get you kids something. This is kinda new to me."

"You've given us more than you realize, John." Jenny's voice was kind of husky. "You gave us hope of a future here."

Soon, we all retired to our beds except Beck. Once, I peeked down over the loft railing. There he sat, in the rocker before the fire, coffee cup in hand, the muffler around his neck. He turned the pocketknife over in his hand. He then watched the fire as he rocked, sipping the coffee. Occasionally he would hold out the knife again and look at it.

He seemed content. That watchful alertness, that taut readiness to meet violence at any instant, was absent. For now, he was a different man. He was a man at peace. It made me sad to think that it was a state that could end at any time.

#

While I settled down to sleep, I noticed a soft sound that I couldn't place. Listening closer, I realized that it came from below in Jenny's room. She was crying.

As I tiptoed down the stairs, Beck's snores rumbled from his room. I knocked lightly on Jenny's door.

"Who is it?" Her voice was low.

"It's me, Sis."

"Come in."

Jenny sat on the edge of the bed, still in her dressing gown. I sat beside her. "What's wrong?"

Tears streamed down Jenny's cheeks. "I miss Momma and Papa."

I put my arm around her. She leaned her head on my shoulder and wept some more. "Yeah, me too." My own eyes were wet and blurry.

After a few minutes, Jenny sat up straight and wiped her eyes. "Well, we must be strong and go on. Trust in the Lord, whatever the circumstances. I'll be all right now. Thank you."

"Good night, Jenny."

"Good night."

I slipped out and returned to my room. Even with two other people in the house, I felt lonely.

Chapter 15

A SUBTLE CHANGE came over the atmosphere of the cabin in the days following Christmas. A sense of lightness and freedom permeated our home, despite cramped quarters. The main flow of this feeling radiated from John Beck. He seemed more relaxed and talkative, less critical, sometimes even jovial. He spent less time brooding over the worn-out wanted posters that he used to read and reread like textbooks. Even the friction that often existed between him and Jenny subsided.

The atmosphere outside had not changed, however. It was not the least bit jovial. Intense, subzero temperatures hung on with bitter tenacity. Occasionally, we'd have a few brief sunny days, soon to be broken by howling gales and snowstorms that might last several hours or several days. Anyone caught out there wouldn't last long.

It was one of those milder mornings that Serenity, the mule-headed, ever-restless mare, found a way to wander off again. Beck had left early to go hunting. I stayed behind, partially to help Jenny with the chores, but more to enjoy a longer time under my warm bed covers.

When I went out to the barn, I found the other horses still in their warm stalls, but the back door stood ajar, and Serenity was missing. When I told Jenny, she groaned and reached for her coat. "I'll go get her." She sighed. "You go ahead and eat your breakfast. I shouldn't be gone long. The tracks will be easy to follow in this snow. If John gets back before I do, tell him what happened."

She was gone a long time. In the three hours after she left, dark, ominous clouds rolled across the sky. Soon, a light snow fell. By afternoon, I decided to saddle my horse and look for her.

As I headed out of the barn, Beck rode up. After I explained the situation, he asked, "When did she leave?"

"About three hours ago."

He squinted up at the sky through the peppering descent of snowflakes and declared, "This snow is gonna get worse. It's probably covered her tracks already. We'll start west beyond the ridge. Stay on my left within the sound of a rifle shot. But move in closer to me if the wind picks up and starts howling. You got that?"

"Yes, sir."

"Remember that one shot means to come together and two means she's been found. Now, let's move out."

The snow did get worse. It came down in thick, white curtains that wiped out all visibility beyond a few feet. The wind roared so that I had to ride close to Beck in order to hear him. Often the horses floundered in troughs of deep snow. The beasts lunged and sank to their bellies, lunged, and sank, and clambered until we urged or coerced them out of the soft traps. Once, we had to get off and help pull them out. Eventually, we took shelter in some rocks.

Toward evening, the snow stopped, and the sky cleared. However, we and the horses were nearly exhausted from our efforts. "We'll spread out and continue the search until sunset, then work our way back home before we freeze to death." Beck scanned the slopes with binoculars. It sent an ominous chill through me to think that Jenny might not return with us.

Our struggles were only partly relieved by the absence of snowfall. There was still the sting of the drifting crystals and the chilling bite of the wind. Yet, something far more threatening became evident. As the sun fell lower, so did the temperature. The wind died down with the light. Without its blanket of clouds, the earth would soon be saturated with the most intense kind of cold. It is that deathly, silent cold that presses down on a living being until it leaves nothing but its own frigid stillness.

Where could Jenny be? There was no sign or sound anywhere. Time and again we called her name only to be answered by silence or the taunting whisper of softly drifting snow. It was as if the storm had carried her out of the world.

Beck and I got off to rest and lead the horses for a while. A sense of desperation appeared to be growing in Beck. "Jenny. Jenny!" he yelled. "She's gotta be out here somewhere. Jenny!" Beck turned in circles, looking through the dusk in every direction, knowing as I did that every moment brought us closer to the point where we would have to give up the search and leave Jenny to the night.

He struggled on, a small figure on an immense mountain slope. He called again without response. Suddenly, he dropped the reins and looked up at the sky. "God." he cried out. "God, if you're up there, show me where to go. I never been what I ought to be and I'm sorry. But I ain't asking for me. Jenny believes in you. She loves you. Now, she's lost and she's dying. Please help me find her."

A moment of silence followed.

"Help me."

Silence.

"Help me!"

The man's voice drifted away into the still evening air, answered only by the mournful howl of a wolf.

The sun was gone.

With a kind of growl, Beck grabbed up the reins and charged on. In a few steps, he stumbled and fell. He pulled himself up on his knees and sat still … terribly still. Then he mounted and turned his horse toward home. Somewhere in the distance a wolf howled a final benediction.

#

Neither of us spoke. A tear froze on my cheek. We were a sad and guilty pair as we trudged toward home, knowing we were leaving Jenny somewhere out there.

If one kind of quiet can be deeper than another, that realm in which Beck rode was the deepest of all. I had never seen him so totally beaten. He was locked in such depth of thought that a gunshot shouldn't bring him out, but something did.

"Trade me horses." He reined his mount to a stop.

"Huh?"

"Give me your horse. You're light. It's not as tired as mine."

"What are you going to do, John?"

"You go on home. I'm going back."

"You haven't got a chance. We looked as far as she could have gone. You said so. The temperature is way below freezing now. You'll get killed yourself."

"Probably, but I got me this crazy idea—the craziest idea I ever had. You remember that story I told you about wolves?"

I nodded.

"Well, it was a bunch of hogwash. I never knew a wolf to attack a man without being prodded into it. But, they are curious animals, and they will follow a person in the woods for miles. I've seen them sit at the edge of my campfires lots o' times, just sitting and watching."

"What does that have to do with Jenny?"

"You remember that wolf we heard howl off on a ridge just beyond where we stopped? I was thinking maybe that wolf followed Jenny to where she holed up. I know it's crazy. There's maybe one chance in a thousand that it'll work out. I sure wouldn't bet money in a poker game on it. But I just gotta go check and see if that wolf is watching somebody."

"Jenny."

Beck and I exchanged horses, then he turned Copper and headed back, a small, lone figure against the vastness of the mountains. He rode straight into the waiting jaws of the great wilderness and disappeared into its depths.

Chapter 16

THE DEEPEST GLOOM pervaded the cabin, untouched by the glow of the crackling fire as I waited. I finally decided to try to sleep, more to forget the ache in my heart than any real weariness.

As I climbed the steps, I prayed for the safety of the two people I cared for most in this world. Yet, it seemed futile, my words going no higher than the ceiling. I gave some thought to how I would survive the winter without them.

Long after I curled up in bed, I drifted off and dreamed of an earlier time. We climbed apple trees in an Indiana orchard. Jenny was just transforming from the best tree-climbing, rock-throwing tomboy in the county into the mysteries of womanhood.

I awoke in the silence of the night, thinking about John Beck and the first day he rode into our valley and all the things he taught us about surviving in the wilderness. Eventually, I drifted back into an uneasy sleep.

Waking the next morning, I hurried down the stairs, calling, "Jenny. John."

Silence.

I shivered, the cabin chillier than it had been in the night. I built up the fire and fixed coffee for people who might never arrive. It was something to do.

I could barely see through the window. I brushed it clear of frost. It had to be almost as cold now as at midnight.

I paced. I checked the coffee. I turned again to the front window and looked through the clear space in the frost. Outside, there was no sign of life, not along the creek, on the ridge, or on the slopes beyond.

Nothing moved, no birds flew over. There were no tracks in the yard of animals passing in the night. Only occasionally did a gust of wind raise great clouds of drifting snow that obscured the clearings and stripped the high cliffs of their winter covering.

The old ticking clock above the mantel labored away the early morning hours. I pondered what I should do about this place. I mean, with just me left.

"God. God help ..." My voice failed.

I wanted to yell or throw something, to protest and declare that everything would be all right. But I couldn't speak. As much as I wanted to, I could no longer deny the reality of the situation. Guilt churned my stomach when I thought of going to town and selling the ranch. That, or trying to stay in this empty cabin, haunted by memories.

Shortly before noon, I glanced out the window and thought I saw something moving across a clearing up on the mountain beyond the ridge. It seemed to be little more than a dot or maybe two close together upon that colossal tapestry of snow.

As I squinted toward the spot, a great burst of wind-driven snow obscured it from view. When the view cleared again, I found nothing in the clearing.

I turned from the window. "Just an elk," I said, the one spark of hope fading within me.

#

It had been some time since I looked out and noticed the dark objects on the mountain slope. My heart leaped as two figures topped the ridge. There were two riders. No ... one walking and leading another on horseback.

"They're coming! Thank you, Lord."

I rushed to get into my coat and boots.

I ran across the yard, snow puffing around my legs as I went. Almost at the creek, I stopped, struck by the approach of the two as they struggled down the slope. Beck trudged ahead through knee-deep snow, leading the horse and its precious burden. Beck stumbled, but he corrected his balance and came straight on. His movements appeared unnatural, mechanical.

I became frightened when they crossed the creek and approached me without a word.

I began to comprehend the hellishness of their ordeal as Beck came close. His face was frozen rock. His mustache and eyebrows were white with frost. He might have been frozen in death except for the proof of his movement and those burning eyes that remained fixed with grim determination on the house. He seemed unaware that I was near. Every fiber of his being was set to that one goal. Reach the cabin.

I hesitated to break his awful concentration with greetings or offers of assistance. Turning my attention to Jenny, my heart sank. Tears welled in my eyes at her pitiful figure upon the exhausted horse. She was still … deathly still. Her head was slumped forward, her face hidden under the folds of her scarf. No sign of strength or life appeared in her. I wondered how she managed to stay on the horse. Then I saw. Her wrists were tied to the saddle horn. Likewise, her legs were tied with a rope stretched under the belly of the animal. Even lifeless, she could not fall from the saddle.

When Beck got to the door, he let the reins drop and just looked at it for a moment. He then turned, dragged the Bowie knife from its sheath and cut the stiff ropes that held Jenny. Though exhausted, he carried her to the door.

He turned toward me, speaking for the first time. "Take care of the horse." With that, he kicked wide the partly open door and entered the cabin. Copper would wait for a few minutes. I had to see if Jenny would be all right.

Once inside, Beck laid Jenny carefully on her bed. She stirred as he spoke her name, slapping her cheeks lightly at the same time. It was as though she were in a deep sleep and didn't want to be disturbed.

"Near froze to death," Beck said. "I'm about played out myself. So you do what I tell you and be quick. See to the horse first, then get me some hot coffee, a lot of it, and two cups. Then heat some water in a pan. Not real hot, just warm."

"Yes, sir."

Beck raised Jenny to sitting position. "Jenny, I'm gonna step outside the door for a bit. You've got to get out of your damp clothes and get into something warm, then cover up with the blankets. Can you do that?"

She nodded.

"Then I'll be back when you're ready."

As we left the room, Beck said, "Have you taken care of the horse yet?"

I shook my head, now remembering my first chore.

"Okay, I'll take care of Copper. He did real well for us out there. You go and fix that hot water and coffee, fast." With that John Beck charged back out into the cold.

#

I hurried to my work. When I returned, Jenny's clothes sat in a pile on the floor. She was wrapped warmly in her flannel nightgown with wool blankets over her. Her hands and feet, left uncovered, had a gray, unhealthy look about them.

John raised her up and gave her some coffee.

"I'm sorry to cause all this trouble." Jenny sounded weak and sleepy. "I was an idiot for going after that silly horse alone."

"Don't talk now. Drink." Beck held the warm cup to her lips, then held one of her hands in his. Next, he had her sit on the edge of the bed and put her feet in the warm water I brought. "You've got a touch of frostbite. Soon you'll feel like your hands and feet are on fire."

"Shouldn't we rub snow on them? I heard a fella back in Indiana say that helps frostbite."

"Easterners." Beck snorted. "We want to warm them up, not get them colder. I once saw a man rub the skin off his fingers trying to git rid of frostbite with snow. No, we want to do this as easy as possible. Not too fast, not too slow."

"They're hurting." Jenny groaned.

"It'll pass. You hang on, Jenny girl." Beck's voice held a tenderness uncommon to him.

The pain became severe. Tears appeared on my sister's cheeks, but she did not cry out. Finally, as Beck had said, the pain subsided. Jenny settled back on the bed and drifted into a natural sleep. She looked small and delicate nestled among the blankets. Her long, dark hair covered the pillow.

"She'll be all right," Beck said. "I'm taking my coffee to my room and going to bed. The first person that disturbs me is gonna get shot."

"Yes, sir." A great weight lifted from me. I wanted to laugh and dance. Instead, I whispered a prayer of thanks.

#

Jenny was the first to wake that evening. She was hungry and grateful for the warm stew I brought to her.

Fed, rested, and still sitting up in bed, she proceeded to tell me about their ordeal.

"When the storm hit, I got lost. My horse lost its footing on a slope and threw me. When I pulled myself out of the snowdrift, the silly beast was gone. I must have wandered in circles for hours. Finally, I took shelter under the low branches of a spruce tree. I tried to start a fire, but seconds after I took off my gloves to light it, my fingers became so stiff I couldn't move them. A pile of snow fell out of the tree on what little flame I had. Finally, I gave up and huddled against the tree trunk. I've never been so cold.

"It's strange, but I eventually began to feel warm and drowsy. I dozed off. I thought I heard a wolf howl once, but I was too tired to be afraid. The next thing I knew, there was John, shaking me and slapping my face, telling me that I was freezing and had to wake up. Then he made a bed of boughs and forced me to eat something. I don't remember what … jerky, I think. The whole time he kept talking to me. I don't remember everything, but he kept telling me to hang on. I wouldn't die. He wouldn't let me. It was all things like that. After working at something for a while, he stretched out beside me. Then, he drew me up against him and pulled his bedroll over us. All I remember after that was feeling warm and, I don't know, safe like when we were children at home."

"Wait, Sis." I hurried out and returned with some more coffee.

She took a sip. "I remember waking once for a moment, feeling warm. He had built a lean-to and a fire.

"Right after sunup, we started back. It was awful. Bitterly cold. Snow kept blowing in my face. Everywhere I looked, nothing in sight for miles but snow. We moved so slowly. After every hour, it seemed we hardly made any progress. I grew tired again, and I knew John was. I tried to get him to stop and rest, but he said we couldn't and just kept plowing on. Finally, everything seemed to be fading. I suppose I might have fallen if John hadn't tied me on the horse. At the time, I couldn't understand why he did such a mean thing. Anyway, I don't remember much in the last few miles until I woke up in my own bed with both of you fussing over me."

"Well, you certainly had me worried, Sis. John was worried, too. Out there on the mountain, he even prayed to find you."

"He did what?" Jenny's eyes widened.

"Well, sort of. Not like you'd hear in church, though."

Jenny fell silent for a long time. "You know …" Her voice soft,

"We've had a hard time getting along with some of John's ways, and he grumbles a lot about what a nuisance we are. But, he cares about us. He cares very much."

"Well, young lady …" Beck stood in the doorway. "You look mighty comfortable. I figured you'd be up cleaning and dusting and complaining about everybody dragging snow in the house by now. By the way, you should be spanked for the trick you pulled, going off alone to look for that fool horse."

"I'm sorry. And I'm much too old to spank." Jenny's eyes twinkled behind her blush.

"Well, I just hope you learned your lesson."

"I'll never do it again. I promise. Now, come here and sit down, please."

The big man sat on a chair beside the bed as Jenny spoke. "We have been talking about the incident and everything you did, and I … I mean …" She smiled, and her eyes became moist. She put her hand on his and tried to convey all her meaning in, "Thank you." For a moment they looked into each other's eyes, and I sensed that something very special passed between them that I could not share.

Then Jenny ordered us out so she could dress and get to cleaning and repairing the mess the house was likely to be in after almost two days without a woman's care. Everyone was happy to return to normalcy. Even Jenny's horse, Maple, returned after another day, hungry and eager for a warm barn. Serenity, however, never returned. Neither did we find her running with any wild horses in the spring.

Chapter 17

WINTER TOOK ITS time sauntering into spring. Our spirits rose with its passage. All mistrust or animosity that had existed between Beck and Jenny dissipated like morning fog. He became settled and less guarded than before. The violence and cautious manner rested deep within him, no longer visible on the outside. For long periods he left his pistol hanging on a peg on the wall. He laughed easily, and sometimes in the evening, he would sit by the fire and tell us stories about earlier days in the West. One night was different. I'll never forget it.

We sat near the fire listening to one of Beck's tales. Jenny gazed into a hand mirror as she brushed her hair.

"After hauling freight for a couple years down in Arizona ..." Beck stirred the coals with a poker. "I hired on as a scout for the army in Arizona. It was a sorry business, though, trying to find the broncos, the wild Apaches, so they wouldn't kill all the whites in the territory. Then trying to keep the peaceful Apaches corralled on a miserable excuse of a reservation so the whites wouldn't kill all of them. Finally, I quit. Since then, I've driven stages, herded cattle, about everything else I reckon. I've met every kind of human being, some of the famous ones included. I played cards with Bill Hickok once over in Dodge City. Some folks say I look like him, but I don't think so. His hair hung down over his shoulders like an Injun's, and he wore his mustache just because his upper lip stuck out. Of the two, I'm by far the better looking." He laughed. We joined in.

"Yes, sir, I done about everything. Not all of it respectable either, I guess. Once I got hired to be the marshal in a boom town called Aurora. The town leaders wanted me to clean out the uncivilized and criminal elements. Then when I finished the job, they fired me for being one of them elements! You know I met yer pa back in the Civil War. We were just green kids ourselves back then, all full of fire and visions of glory." He chuckled. "Thought we were gonna win that whole thing in two weeks." Beck turned serious. "Civil War, there ain't anything *civil* about war. We found that out real fast. Had so many close calls I don't know how we made it out alive. There's nothing like seeing a thousand men rushing across a field all bent on killing you. Fellas you know dying all around you. The two of us probably saved each other's lives a half-dozen times, I reckon."

Beck twisted the corner of his mustache. "Things like that bring men together in a bond like nothing else. So, we just stuck together after the war. Him and me wandered around, even prospected here in Colorado for a couple years before we made a strike that was worth anything. I finally bought a ranch with my share. It was just a small spread, but I liked it." He sighed. "It didn't work out, though."

He fell silent for a long time and watched Jenny brushing her hair. She sat in dreamy meditation as the brush drifted down in slow strokes through the long, soft strands that fell like a heavy curtain about her shoulders.

"You remind me of my wife, sitting there now the way you are," Beck said. "She was young and pretty and mighty proud of her hair. She would sit by the bed at night and take ever so long to comb her hair until it was kitten soft and glass smooth. Her hair was long like yours but black, blue-black as a winter night."

"I didn't know you were married," Jenny said with great interest.

"Yeah, I met her just after I started the ranch and turned respectable." Beck smiled. "Her name was Maria. I guess she was the most gentle woman I ever knew. Wouldn't hardly kill flies." His expression turned dark as he stared into the fire. "We had been married about a year when she told me she was in the family way. Like a fool, I went to town to celebrate. When I returned, I found the tracks of three riders in the front yard. They were probably saddle tramps, not men drifting between jobs, but the kind that make their money by robbing lone travelers or houses where nobody's home. They may have asked to water their horses and figured out pretty quick that there was no man around. I called for Maria as I ran into the house." He shook his head. "She was dead and the house was ransacked."

John paused with a sigh, then went on. "She went out game,

though. I kept an old pistol in the dresser drawer. She got off a couple shots, nicked one of them before they gunned her down." He glanced over at us, his eyes moist, then quickly looked back at the fire. "Their trail led through Texas and Colorado. I almost caught them in Utah. It was nearly a year after I started that I followed them up into Wyoming."

He went silent again, so with youthful eagerness that I now regret, I asked, "What happened?"

Without turning his intense gaze from the fire, he said, "I found them." That was the last he ever said about the subject.

#

Jenny sat in a rocking chair on the porch, taking advantage of some sunshine as she darned a pair of my socks. She paused and looked out across our land. "You know, Dave, for the first time, I feel like we are really going to make it. We are going to turn this into a fine ranch ... a real home."

"Yeah, me too." I leaned against the porch post, enjoying my morning coffee before I joined Beck down at the creek with my fishing pole.

"John has taught us so much."

"He sure has."

Jenny watched as Beck caught a fish. "Do you think John is handsome?"

"What?" I nearly choked on a swig of coffee at the unexpected question.

"You know, in a rugged sort of way."

"Well ... I don't know. I never thought about it."

Jenny took a couple stitches with the needle and thread.

"Sis, are you getting sweet on Beck?"

"Oh, no!" She wrinkled her nose. "Of course not."

Another moment of silence ensued.

"It's just that I think, down deep, John is a good man, but he carries a lot of pain inside. I just wish that he could be happy again. Maybe if he found a nice wife ..."

"Why are women always trying to find wives for men?"

She chuckled. "It's in our natures, I guess."

"I don't think he will find one around here." I finished my last swallow of coffee.

Jenny frowned as she went back to her work.

#

Our peace was broken one day by a single, unsettling incident. Travel was still difficult in early spring because of the lingering patches of snow in shadowed areas, some of which were rather deep. We were, therefore, surprised to see a lone rider coming off the ridge. The horse waded through snow and the creek, kicking up sprays of water and ice crystals as it came.

Any expectation we had of a friendly visit disappeared when we recognized Frank Maxwell. He offered no greeting but stared at us with a look as cold as the icy creek. "It's been a rough winter. I see you all made it." He stared at the three of us standing before our door.

"Yep." Beck spit over the edge of the porch.

"You ready to talk about selling?" Frank turned to me.

"Nope."

Without another word, Frank Maxwell turned and rode away. An uneasy feeling stirred in me after this unusual event.

"I can't believe that he rode all the way over here just to exchange a half dozen words." Jenny put her fists on her hips.

I turned to Beck. "I don't like it. I think he was hoping we were all dead."

Beck said nothing at all, but a little later, I noticed that he wore his gun again.

Chapter 18

Joe Warner leaned back on the seat of his freight wagon after reining his horses to a stop outside our cabin. "Howdy, folks."

"Good morning, Mr. Warner." Jenny wiped her hands on a dish towel. "What brings you out so early?"

"Circuit ridin' preacher is comin' to do a sermon this Sunday. I'm passin' the word around. He'll do baptisms and weddin's, too, for anybody that wants them. They say the preacher is young but loud, right entertainin'."

"Where will the service be held?"

"On that hill just behind the saloon. Or in the saloon if it rains."

"Then we will just have to pray for a bright sunny day. We'll be happy to come." Jenny smiled, her eyes fairly sparkling with excitement as she looked over at me. "Won't we?"

"Aw, Sis, I planned to go fishing after devotions on Sunday."

"Not this Sunday, young man. You'll do better to receive food for the soul from a fisher of men." She looked back up at Joe. "We'll be there."

"That'll be fine. Oh, by the way, there will be a picnic after the service. Bring enough food to share."

"That sounds wonderful!" Jenny clapped her hands.

"Yep." Joe nodded. "This thing's turnin' into a real shindig."

I kicked a pebble off the porch and watched Jenny as she turned toward John, who stood in the doorway with a cup of coffee. He lifted his cup. "Coffee, Joe?"

"No, thanks. Got to finish gittin' the word out and pick up a shipment for the store. So long. See you folks at the Sunday meetin'."

He gave the reins a snap and headed the horses off on his rounds.

When Jenny and I turned to go in, Beck was just putting his empty cup on the table. "I trust you're going with us, John." Jenny picked up the cup and took it aside to clean.

"Where?"

"Church, of course."

John shook his head. "Nope."

Jenny raised an eyebrow. "And why not?"

"Too dangerous."

"Now how can going to church be dangerous?"

"Well, y' see, if God saw me walk into a group of all those good holy folks, He might get so riled that He would just strike me with lightning. With so many people close around me, some might get hit, too. Several people could get killed. We sure wouldn't want that to happen."

I laughed, but Jenny stomped her foot. "John Beck, that's the silliest excuse I ever heard!"

Beck held out his hands and shrugged. "I'm just thinking about the welfare of others."

"I am going to my room right now and pray that the good Lord will shake some sense into you." My sister marched toward her room with determination. She was on a mission.

"The Lord and I haven't seen eye to eye in some time, missy. So, plan on making it one of those earthshaking, heaven-moving prayers. None of those little everyday prayers."

She turned in midstride with a confident smile. "I can do that."

I nodded to Beck. "Yep, she can do that if anybody can."

He turned to me with a chuckle and a wink.

#

One of Jenny's prayers was answered. That Sunday was bright with a crystal blue and cloudless sky. Sunlight shimmered off the sparkling snow on the mountain peaks. A brisk breeze made our light jackets feel comfortable.

When we arrived, men scurried about, moving chairs from the saloon onto the grassy hill so the older folks wouldn't have to sit on the ground. Others spread blankets. Some of the ladies set covered dishes on tables adorned with colorful cloths.

"This is truly the day the Lord hath made!" Jenny fairly vibrated with joy. I reined our horses to a stop as the wagon creaked. I tied those horses to a stake near the others in an outer circle of the meadow. Around us, the foothills of the mountains formed a natural amphitheater that would carry the voice of the preacher to the whole valley.

I spread our blanket. It was big enough for Jenny and me ... and John, if he had come. Around us, I noticed several of the townspeople and homesteaders. Joe Warner waved to me, and I waved in return. Cattlemen and miners tended to sit toward the back of the crowd.

As I looked to the front, my stomach turned. Frank Maxwell stood before us next to a man I assumed to be the minister. Jenny and I glanced at each other. "How did that fox get in the henhouse?" I whispered.

Maxwell removed his white Stetson. "Ladies and gentlemen, neighbors and friends, it gives me great honor to introduce the Reverend Thomas Worthington, who will share from his heart the word of the Lord. But first, Sister Bertha Malloy has kindly agreed to lead us in a hymn. Mrs. Malloy?"

A stocky woman in a blue checked dress and bonnet stepped forward. "Let us now stand and sing that glorious song, 'Rock of Ages.'"

A conglomeration of off-key tones sounded. "Rock of ages, cleft for me, let me hide myself in Thee." Finally, Mrs. Malloy concluded with, "You may be seated."

The impromptu congregation settled into an attentive silence as the minister stepped up behind a simple makeshift lectern. He was young for a preacher, as Joe had said, seventeen, maybe eighteen at most. "Greetings brothers and sisters in the name of our Lord Jesus Christ!" As promised, his voice echoed loud across the valley. "Let us praise Him in this glorious day." Worthington lifted his Bible and waved it about. "Rejoice in the midst of this mighty natural cathedral created by the hand of the great God Almighty, himself." A breeze tousled the man's shock of dark brown hair.

A number of nods and *amens* resounded from the people. I straightened a fold in our blanket as I glanced with longing at the food basket behind us. When I looked over at Jenny, I noticed that my sister never took her eyes from the handsome young preacher.

Reverend Worthington opened his Bible. "Those of you who have your Bibles, please turn with me to this day's text, Romans chapter six, verse twenty-three. And if one is sitting near you without The Book, kindly share yours with them."

Jenny held out our old family Bible, worn with years of use and filled with generations of names of the Foster family tree. We leaned close together where I could read with her. That Good Book always moved me with a sense of awe whenever I looked into its yellowed pages.

The minister began, "For the wages of sin is death; but the gift of God is eternal life through Jesus Christ our Lord." Worthington held out the Holy Book as if offering it to us. "Folks, we live in a fallen world, and we are all sinners. If we don't have the forgiveness and grace of God, we are without hope." He held up the Book. "Woe to those who are bound for a fiery hell!"

"Amen," and, "Preach it, Brother!" echoed from members of the audience.

"Tell 'em who's gonna be in hell, young man," demanded one woman in a strident voice.

"Well, uh ..." the young parson seemed taken off guard at the vocal response. "Thieves and murderers."

"Who else? Who else?"

The minister appeared to search the sky for his list. "Um, those given to the gambling trade. Those sold out to hard liquor. And, and lewd women."

At that moment, a deep male voice rumbled out from the back of the crowd, "Oh, death, where is thy sting?"

Several of the ladies responded with audible huffs at the misinterpreted scripture while some gentlemen struggled to stifle a chuckle. But the crowd at the back exploded with loud guffaws that finally infected most of the congregation.

The poor, embarrassed preacher's face glowed red in the clear mountain sunlight. He looked heavenward for direction. In a moment, he turned back to the people, and he laughed. "Yep, you kind of got me there. I see some of you would agree with the saying that heaven is for climate, but hell is for company."

More chuckles.

The preacher shook his head, and a look of sadness came over his face that gave him the appearance of one much older. "I am sorry from the depths of my heart to tell you that there will be no laughter in hell. Never again will there be the sound of laughter or words of love or words of comfort from a friend or mother. Only screams and unheeded begging in fires that burn without light. The only company will be the wailing of other poor wretches out in the darkness."

It became very quiet in that valley then. I pulled my jacket a little tighter.

"But that's why I'm here, my friends." Thomas lifted his Bible as if holding something precious. "I came to tell you that this is not where the verse ends. It goes on, 'but the gift of God is eternal life through Jesus Christ our Lord.' No one has to go to the place of punishment we deserve for the sins we have done or thought or desired. Jesus gives us a second chance."

Somebody sniffed behind me.

"Jesus loved us enough to take our death and punishment for us on the cross. It's like ... an outlaw aimed a Colt.45 at your heart, and Jesus stepped in front of the gun and took the bullet for you. Now, there's a friend. All to give you life, real life forever." He took a deep breath. "And heaven ... more beautiful than what we see around us today." Worthington waved his hands toward the mighty peaks.

"Laughter? There'll be lots of laughter ... thousands of voices breaking out in in sheer joy." The preacher laughed himself as if at the thought of it. "But I'll tell you what there won't be. There will be no sorrow, no pain or aging, no regrets, no fear. You townsfolk, there'll be no fear of being robbed. Every stranger will instantly be a friend. You cowmen, no fear of being trampled to pieces under a thousand stampeding cattle. You miners, no fear of cave-ins. No varmints or dangerous animals. Why, there you can play with a mountain lion like a kitten."

Down the row from me, an old cowhand with a handlebar mustache wiped his nose on a bandana.

"Best of all, friends, you'll feel really loved like you've never felt it before. Forgiven and free and loved by God. Love greater than anything you've felt since your mother first held you in her arms."

Pastor Worthington stepped in front of the lectern with his hands out at his sides, his voice softer now. "It's all a free gift. Just come forward and ask Jesus to forgive you and be your Lord and to guide you through that new life. Come now as Sister Malloy leads in a closing hymn."

Mrs. Malloy led everyone in several choruses of "Bringing in the sheaves. Bringing in the sheaves. We shall come rejoicing, bringing in the sheaves." Eight men and three women went forward to pray with the preacher. One fellow dressed in miner's work clothes tossed a whiskey bottle into the brush as he walked. Later, another man slipped over to find the bottle then toss it away after discovering it was empty.

The repentant then headed over to an icy stream for a quick baptism. Right after that three couples were married. One pair was old, somewhere around forty, I guessed.

"Well, this has been real church." Jenny smiled at me. "Aren't you glad we came?"

"Yeah, I suppose so." I didn't want to sound overly eager to my sister. However, the day did bring to my mind a fond memory of a day back in Indiana. As we sat by the river, kindly old Reverend Fred Winfrey laid down his fishing pole and led me through that special prayer many of these folks had said today.

"David, get out the food while I go pay my respects to the minister." Jenny hurried over to Reverend Worthington as I went for the food basket. I carried it to one of the tables near where Jenny and the preacher stood within earshot over the crowd. The preacher said, "I wish I could stay, but I have many other towns to cover. It may be six months before I get back this way."

Jenny sighed, giving the fellow a big cow-eyed smile as she said, "You will be in our prayers as you are on your journey. And … you will be welcome, sir, to join us for a meal in our humble home whenever you are passing through this area."

Worthington smiled back. "Thank you, Miss Foster. I would be honored."

I placed our food, including one of Jenny's apple pies, on the community table when Frank Maxwell stepped up to her and Worthington, his voice jovial and booming louder than the preacher's had been

"Hello, Miss Foster." He tipped his hat. "You look well today."

"Thank you, Mr. Maxwell." My sister's voice conveyed a cold politeness.

Maxwell turned to Worthington. "That was a fine sermon, Parson, a fine sermon, indeed. I say amen. You are what this territory needs to become part of a civilized land."

"Thank you, sir, but it is the Spirit of the Lord that wins the souls of the people. I just share His words."

"Indeed, indeed. And those words have truly moved me today. May God bless you in your continued work. Good day, sir." He nodded to Worthington and tipped his hat again to Jenny before moving on to speak to another couple.

I never expected that Frank Maxwell was a religious man. Could I have been wrong about him having something to do with my father's death? If not him … who?

Jenny and I returned to the blanket with our lunch when a rider on the ridge above the valley caught my attention. It was John Beck. He remained motionless a minute longer, then turned his mount and rode away, disappearing into the pines.

Chapter 19

FISHING WAS NEVER just about catching fish. To me it was the magic of the streams. The gurgling laughter of water dancing over rocks below rugged cliffs rising to the songs of birds. It's hard to put the feel of it in words, I reckon.

That's the anticipation I felt as I explored a section of the creek I had not covered before. That and the joy of the game, trying to catch a creature divinely designed to avoid capture. The sudden tautness at the end of a slender line and the bend-to-near-breaking of a limber willow pole. The battle to get a fighting fish to the shore from its mysterious, hidden home in the depths.

I dismounted and tied my horse to a white-barked aspen. Slipping slowly and as quietly as possible through the trees, hoping to avoid detection by my wary prey, I eased my way toward the bank.

"Yahoo!"

I jerked straight up, startled at the sound of another human voice in that secluded place. Again, by stealth, as Beck had taught me, I stepped carefully to keep from breaking any twigs underfoot. Peering around a tree, I spied a man wading up from the water, holding a large, struggling fish and a strange looking fishing pole. It was Frank Maxwell. I started to turn and hurry away.

Glancing up, he saw me and held up the fish. "Ah, young Mr. Foster, what do you think of this fine fellow?"

I turned and stepped around the tree. "It's big."

He laughed. "Indeed, it is, my boy! Indeed, it is."

Now, I planted my feet. "You know you're on our land?"

"Oh, come on, son. You wouldn't deny a man a few fish from your part of the creek, would you? What kind of neighbor would that be?"

"Well. . . I suppose not."

"It is such an outstanding day for fishing, I lost track as I worked my way upstream until I came upon this teeming pool." He laid the fish down and removed the hook, then placed the still flopping creature into a kind of wicker basket with a lid.

The odd pole he used drew my attention. A long rod attached to a handle of what appeared to be cork. At the back end of the handle sat a round metal wheel that fed out line through small rings along the length of the pole.

"What kind of rig is that?" I sat on a log.

"This?" He held up the pole. "This is called a fly fishing rod. They're real popular in the British Isles and just starting to be seen back East. I had this one imported from England."

"How do you work it?" I grew interested.

"Step over here, boy, and I'll show you." He beckoned me with a wave of his hand.

I walked nearer.

Maxwell waded into the water. "You see, you feed some line out through the rings along the pole from the reel at the back. Then, with your elbow against your side, lift the rod up like going around a clock to the eleven o'clock position. Pull up fast to the one o'clock position. That casts the line behind you." With a flick, the line straightened out behind the man.

"Now, cast it forward until it shoots out over the water just where you want it. Let the fuzzy lure on the end of the line drop real gentle, like a fly lighting on the surface." The line and lure did just as he instructed.

"Now, you try it." I stepped into the chilly water until it was up to my knees. Maxwell handed me the rod. I flinched a little when he placed one hand on my shoulder and one on my wrist.

"Remember, elbow against your side, rod at eleven o'clock. Now back to one o'clock. Feel it stretch out behind you. Now, forward."

I flung the pole out, causing the line to slap the water in a messy bunch.

"You went too far forward. Stop as you get back to eleven o'clock. Try again."

This time, as I cast the line forward, it didn't come. However, I felt the rod bend in the opposite direction from where I wanted it to go.

Maxwell laughed. "Davy, my boy, you caught yourself a fine big aspen tree!" He detached the lure from the stem of a leaf. "Always be aware of where your fly is going. Many a fisherman has caught more trees than fish at first. This time, turn and watch to make sure the line stretches out in an open space. Also, when you get back to eleven o'clock, give the rod a thrust ahead like you're going to pound a nail with a hammer into a board straight ahead of you."

"It's sure not as easy as you make it look, Mr. Maxwell."

"Time and patience, boy, time and patience." Maxwell sighed. "Try again."

This time I concentrated on all Maxwell had told me. Backward, forward to eleven o'clock, thrust the hammer. The line arched and unfurled gracefully over the water, dropping softly to the surface.

"That's it. You've got it," Maxwell spoke in a near whisper. "Now, just let the fly drift with the current past that big bolder."

I watched the lure float delicately on the water. Suddenly, a splash, and water droplets glistened in the sun.

"Jerk, boy, set the hook!"

The rod bent almost double with the power of the fish.

"You've got a big one. Let him take some line. When he stops tugging, pull or reel it in. Keep working him. Don't let him get away." Maxwell's excitement seemed as great as mine.

The fish and I fought back and forth for several minutes.

"Careful, don't let it get into that brush. He'll break the pole. Pull hard, now."

I pulled hard, the rod bending dangerously low again. Finally, I could sense the fish getting tired.

My fishing partner grabbed a fancy net made of a rich red and blond cedar wood. Wading out into the water, he swept up my prize.

I nearly jumped with delight. "Whoo-wee, that's a big one, isn't it!"

"Sure is. And you did it yourself."

"With your help. I do thank you, Mr. Maxwell."

"Think nothing of it, my young friend. You've got the makings of a real fly fisherman." The man handed me my fish. I held its cold wet body in my hands admiring its brown, gold and red spots.

"Yep, that trout, along with mine, will make a tasty meal. Makes me hungry just to look at them. What do you say to fixing them right now for our lunch?"

"Well … sure."

As Maxwell cleaned the fish on a flat-topped rock, I started a small fire. Soon our catch roasted on sticks. We sat on a log. Our conversation, as we ate, revolved around fishing and Maxwell's newfangled fishing pole. I relished the smoky taste of the freshly cooked fish while we talked.

"So, you really like this fly rod?"

"Yeah, I sure do. Maybe someday, when our ranch gets to paying, I'll buy me one."

"Here, take this one." Maxwell handed me the pole.

"Really?"

"Yep."

"No, that's too much. I couldn't take something this nice without paying."

"Nah, don't worry about it. I have three more at home. Just think of it as a neighborly gift."

"Gee! I don't know what to say. Thank you."

"You're welcome. Besides, what are neighbors for?"

As I admired the fishing rod, Maxwell hesitated a few seconds then continued. "Davy, I'm real sorry about your father. I didn't get to know him well, but I could see that he was a fine man."

"Thanks." I felt a huskiness in my voice.

"I know how you feel. I know what is to lose family."

I didn't respond.

"I had the start of a good farm." Maxwell removed his Stetson, wiped his brow and set the hat on his knees. He rubbed the brim as he looked out beyond the creek. "Southern raiders-turned-outlaws attacked my home one night. In the fight, they killed my wife and boy, burned my house and anything they couldn't carry with them. Left me for dead."

More silence.

With a shake of his head and a half-smile Maxwell said, "Sally had the blondest hair I ever saw, like spun gold." He gave a slight laugh. "And that boy of mine ... Yes, sir, that boy sure loved to fish."

"How old was he?"

"Six. Just six years old when ..."

I looked away from the pain in the man's eyes as he gazed into the distance as if looking into the past.

He put his hat back on. The tone of his voice turned hard. "Then and there, I vowed that nobody would ever take anything away from me again. From then on, I would do the taking."

I fingered the fishing pole, feeling a heaviness in my heart.

"You know what, Davy? I just had a thought. I got no kin, nobody to leave anything to, and I've taken a liking to you. If you would sell your ranch to me, legal, you could come work for me. I'd treat you like my own son. Start you out as a hand, train you up to foreman someday. Then, when I die, I'll leave it all to you. You'll have your ranch and mine, the biggest ranch in the state. What do you say?"

I arched my eyebrows and scratched my chin. "Uh. . . I don't know. I'm not sure what Jenny would think about that."

"Well, I'll just hire her, too. I bet she's a good cook, right?"

"Yeah, she is."

"So, there you are. This'll be great! I'll fire that Mexican chili burner I got now, and we will make a great team."

My head spun. This all came too fast. "What about Jud Sykes?"

"What about him?"

"I don't like him. I don't want him around."

"Oh, Jud is all right once you get to know him. He can be kinda cantankerous at times, but I control him. I'll see he goes easy on you. Besides, I need him. He handles certain awkward problems for me."

Control seemed to be a driving motivation of Maxwell's whole being. "I got to think about it. Maybe I'll just pray on it a while."

Maxwell gave a sarcastic sounding laugh. "Don't waste your time praying and thinking. Take this opportunity now, or you'll miss out."

"What do you mean? Don't you pray about things? You go to church. I saw you."

"Well, now, going to church is all right. It's a way to get in good with prominent citizens with upstanding reputations. Especially if a man is looking at someday becoming governor. But make no mistake, son, there's no God. No pie in the sky by and by. There's just power here and now. Land makes money, and money makes power. Come in with me, and I'll teach you how to get it."

I furrowed my brow. "Don't. . . don't you want a decent life with a nice wife and family again?"

The man shook his head. "One way or another, that only comes to pain. Besides, I've got a half-breed woman that comes over to take care of my needs. She gets paid well. Everybody is satisfied. No love, no commitments, no problems."

I stood. "I've got to go."

"I know what!" Maxwell's face lit up. "She's got a younger sister, a couple years or so older than you. Give me the word, and I'll introduce you to her. Oh, boy, she can teach you some things that will make you howl with delight."

Heat radiated through my face like spreading fire.

Maxwell laughed. "Why, my boy, I believe you're blushing. Well, no matter. When you grow up, and you have those urges, let me know, and I'll fix you up."

"No."

His words became stern. "Don't be a fool, boy. I won't offer you these opportunities twice. Join me, and you can have it all, everything you ever dreamed of and more."

A chill went through me, clear to the depth of my soul. The words of Satan in the Bible came to my memory of when he said to Jesus, "Bow down before me, and I will give you all the kingdoms of the earth."

All I wanted was to get far away.

"If you don't take this offer, you'll regret it, boy."

I don't know how it worked, but there seemed to be darkness and fire at the same time in Maxwell's eyes. I turned to go.

"Nobody walks away from me."

I leaned his fishing rod against a tree. Mounting my horse, I looked back at him. "I'm sorry about your family."

I walked the horse away, but once out of Maxwell's sight, kicked it to a gallop. When I got to the ridge above our ranch, I stopped and just looked at it for several minutes. It looked so good and peaceful and … safe.

I did, however, glance back down the creek where I had left Maxwell. I gave a sigh. I sure did like that fishing rod.

Chapter 20

WITH THE FULLNESS of spring, the mountains burst to overflowing with life and color. New growth in shades of bright green tipped the pine and spruce trees. The new leaves on the aspens were so light in color they appeared to form a pale green mist in the distance. The hills bloomed with the radiance of a million flowers, the bold red of Indian paintbrush, and the soft blue of mountain columbines. The air was alive with the music of returning birds.

"It's too beautiful to stay indoors," Jenny declared one day. "Let's take a picnic lunch up on the mountain."

It took little persuasion to get the rest of us to agree. Soon we seated ourselves on a blanket in a flower-carpeted meadow high above the cabin. The cool, clear air of the higher altitude stimulated our appetites. Fried chicken, biscuits with butter and honey, and fresh-baked dried apple pie satisfied our hunger.

After lunch, Beck stretched out for a snooze in the sun while Jenny went for a walk. She tried to convince him that the exercise of a walk would be good for him. "I'll just exercise my mind in deep thought," he said. Deep sleep appeared to be his more likely goal.

Meanwhile, I tried out my newly cut fishing pole in a nearby stream. With the droning of insects and the babbling of the rocky stream, I grew drowsy when a movement behind me caught my attention. Jenny returned from her walk, carrying a bouquet of wildflowers. She had a mischievous look in her eyes as she watched Beck sleeping.

"Winter is over. It's time to come out of hibernation," she said. There was no response. "John, wake up and look at my flowers."

"They're real pretty," he mumbled without raising his hat from his eyes.

Jenny now changed her tactics. After waiting several seconds, she knelt beside the drowsing man and touched a flower stem to his chin. He moved slightly. She leaned over and tickled his ear. He swatted the air and scratched the apendage. It was all Jenny could do to stifle her giggles.

When she touched his chin again, Beck spoke from under his hat. "If somebody doesn't stop bothering me, I'm gonna throw that person in the stream."

Jenny couldn't resist the temptation, though, and soon repeated her actions. Beck leaped to his feet, roaring like a bear. Jenny screamed and tried to run, but it was futile. In an instant, Beck caught her, hauled her up over his shoulder and carried her toward the stream.

"John, no. Help, Dave. Aaaah!" Jenny screamed, kicking and squirming in a vain attempt to escape.

I joined into the game with mock bravado. "Villain! Unhand that fair maiden." I charged like a jousting knight.

"Stop me if you think you're big enough," Beck challenged.

An unsettling realization struck me. I was all that stood between them and the stream. I had no illusions that I could pit my size and strength against that of John Beck. Yet, I was determined to give it my best effort. Head and shoulders lowered, I rammed into Beck's legs. To my great surprise, Beck, still holding Jenny, crumpled to the ground with me on top. The whole pile of us remained where we fell and laughed, but none more heartily than John Beck.

"I didn't know you had it in you, Dave." He chuckled. "Yes, sir, all the tough hombres better walk soft when you're around."

"I knew I wouldn't be thrown in the stream," Jenny said with confidence. "Dave couldn't do it alone, and you, Mr. Beck, are too much of a gentleman." She then took the bouquet of flowers, shook them in Beck's face, and ran away again.

After such an insult to our prowess, I ran after her too. She nimbly danced across the stream on some flat rocks. Beck just plowed through the chilly, knee-deep water. It took him only two steps to cross.

Jenny disappeared around a large spruce. When Beck and I came around the tree, she stood staring toward the north, the flowers slipping from her hand.

Thick black smoke rose from the direction of the cabin. We all ran. Once, through an opening in the trees, I caught a glimpse of horsemen near the cabin. We advanced to the foot of the slope, still running. By the time we reached the clearing, the riders disappeared over the ridge.

Both the cabin and the barn were on fire. Beck grabbed a shovel that leaned against the garden fence and threw dirt on the flames lapping up the logs of our house. I rushed into the barn to let out the horses, and then grabbed buckets, harness, and as much equipment as I could carry before the heat and flames became too intense. Jenny took the buckets to the creek for water.

We made a bucket relay between creek and cabin, having given up the barn to the flames. I scooped up buckets of water and ran to Jenny. She passed them to Beck, who stood dangerously close to the burning porch and front wall, dowsing them with the water.

Soon, we drowned the last sparks. We had arrived in time to save the cabin, the damage relatively minor, being almost as much from water as from flames.

The barn was lost, however. It quickly billowed into a blazing pyre and collapsed with a deafening explosion of sparks into a pile of glowing rubble.

Beck sat on the ground staring at the buildings, muttering curses. I went inside our cabin with Jenny to clean up the mess. The thick log walls had kept most of the flames outside.

Suddenly, Beck yelled, "Dave! Help me round up the horses. We're goin' huntin' for rats."

Chapter 21

THE TRACKS OF horses led toward Goldstrike. We went straight to the saloon and dismounted next to the four horses hitched to the rail. The lights inside emitted a smoky yellow glow through the windows. The quiet of the dusk reigned over the saloon, as it was still too early for the majority of its patrons to arrive.

"We'll try to do this without gunplay," Beck said. "It was a small barn anyway. The way Maxwell takes having his men roughed up will give us an idea how far he's willing to take this thing."

Jenny looked through the window. "John, there's four of them in there,"

"Yeah, won't be much of a fight at all." Beck hitched up his belt. "Jenny, just in case, you stand right outside the door with the rifle pointed in. Lever it once after I get inside so everybody will know there's a gun on 'em."

"What do you want me to do?" I asked.

"Stay with the horses."

"Stay with the horses! It's always 'stay with the horses,'" I grumbled to myself, all the while having every intention of slipping in the door the moment the action started.

As I looked in from the outside, the saloon was small and delapidated. Two other doors opened into the back room and the side alley. The bartender wiped glasses behind a plain wooden bar. I noticed the only decoration was a faded picture of a scantily clad woman on the wall. Of six tables, only two were occupied. Two men, townsmen, sat at a table on the right side of the room while four cowmen played cards at a table on the left.

"What'll it be?" asked the bartender as Beck stepped up to the bar.

"Nothing, thanks. I just come hunting some rats that got in our barn today. Clumsy varmints. They caught it on fire."

A low chuckle rumbled from the left side of the room. It ended with the clear, unmistakable sound of a rifle being levered just beyond the door.

"Yes, sir, I had a feeling they might have a nest in here. And I was right." Beck turned and looked straight at Maxwell's four men.

They were a surly-looking group. Jud Sykes appeared the meanest, no matter who he was with. One man had a full beard. Another had red hair and a missing tooth. The fourth was nearly bald, with more hair below his nose than on his head. They all watched Beck with cautious hostility. One looked over at the rifle barrel sticking through the doorway.

The two townsmen left quietly.

"Now you don't have to waste bullets on rats. You just beat all the wind out of 'em, and there ain't nothing left," Beck declared. "Ain't that right, rats?" No answer. He then shook his head and said, "Well, let's git to it!"

An immediate explosion of movement came in answer. A chair flew at Beck, who ducked and caught the first two assailants with a vicious uppercut and a right hook.

The chair hit the bartender and the picture. He, the immodest lady, and the chair all dropped behind the bar. In a moment, the bartender scrambled back up, wielding an ax handle. He tried to take a swing at Beck, but the big man glimpsed the move, caught the arm in midswing, and felled him with a single punch that sent the bartender into sweet repose for the remainder of the festivities.

Watching from the front door, I got so excited, I lunged into battle myself. The bald cowman stood with his back toward me, preparing to dive back into the pandemonium that centered on Beck.

With a wild yell, I charged. I intended to kick his leg out from under him, then jump on top and pulverize my victim with a barrage of flying punches. However, just as I got within range, he spun around, and my kick caught him between the legs. To my surprise, he yelped and hobbled over to a chair in the corner to sit out the next dance. He glared at me with a look very similar to that of the grizzly bear I'd met the previous fall.

As I turned back into the fray, a flying chair caught me head on and sent me hurling through the swinging doors in a rolling blur of thrashing arms and chair legs. I had quite a tussle with that chair until I kicked free and headed back into the saloon.

As soon as I waded in, someone grabbed me by the seat of my pants and my shirt collar and threw me into the street. Dusting myself off, I started back in, but Jenny grabbed me to hold me back. Just then, a bottle crashed into the doorframe by our heads, and I decided to continue only as a spectator.

Jud traded punches with Beck. Both looked exhausted, blood and bruises decorating their faces. Finally, Jud swung a kick at John, who moved enough to make it ineffectual and left Jud off balance. Beck moved in with a right cross. Jud staggered back. Beck swung a left just a bit harder, weakening his opponent more. Finally, he mustered all his effort into a right cross that sank Jud to the floor, cold.

Just then, the redhead grabbed Beck and spun him around to give him a big roundhouse punch. But, before he could swing, John grabbed him and swung a mighty right cross that sent the man flying across the room. The hombre tumbled over tables and chairs into an unconscious heap in the corner.

Now Beck was in trouble. Baldy and the bearded one came at him from opposite sides, and Beard Face grabbed him from behind while the bald one swung a left and a right to his face, followed by a brutal punch to the stomach. Beck seemed to weaken, but then with a ferocious growl and a great heave, he whirled around, shaking the bearded man loose and throwing him against the other. As the two cowmen worked their way to their feet for another attack, Beck picked up the ax handle from the bar where it had fallen and swung it backhanded into the face of the first assailant, felling him like a tree. The second man, ducking too late, took the force of the two-handed swing of the club. It struck with a resounding crack, and John Beck stood alone in the midst of bodies and debris.

Jenny came in and stepped to the left of the doorway to view the aftermath, the rifle held loosely now in her hands.

All seemed finished when a young, sandy-haired cowman stepped in through the saloon doors. A solid toughness permeated his look and the way he moved.

"What's going on here?" He turned to Beck. "I take it you're responsible for all this."

Beck looked around and answered with a pleased, "Yep."

"I work with these men," the stranger said.

"That's your mistake, son."

"You got something against the Maxwell outfit?"

"Nothing except that they work for a crook."

"Those are riling words about the man that keeps me fed."

"He could get you killed," Beck said with cold seriousness.

"Maybe yer the man who thinks he's going to do that killing," the younger man said. The whole atmosphere once again filled with tension. A hint of that deadly game played over a campfire the preceding autumn seeped into the air.

"Stop this, both of you!" Jenny stomped into the room. "This is going too far. Mr. Dawson, these men burned our barn. We followed their trail here."

"You know him?" Beck asked with surprise.

"Yes, this is Luke Dawson. He is the young man who stopped by looking for work last fall while you were hunting." She turned to the young man. "This is John Beck, a friend of my family. He helped my brother and me through the winter."

Dawson turned to Jenny and said, "I didn't mean to cause you alarm, Miss Foster. Naturally, I was caught off guard when I walked into this mess." He then turned to Beck. "I don't hold with barn-burning, an' I reckon these fellas got what they deserved. So it looks like you and I haven't got any more business here."

"That suits me," Beck said, "but I expect there'll be more trouble like this, maybe gunplay. I hope you won't have to get mixed up in it."

Luke took a long look at John Beck and then said, "I'll decide what's best to do when the time comes." With that, he tipped his hat to Jenny and left through the front doors. He wore his gun tied down as Beck did.

Beck turned to the bartender, who had come to. "The rats here will pay for the damages," he said as we left.

We had no more than stepped out on the walk when we ran into Frank Maxwell himself. Just as he said, "Well, Mr. Beck," Beck flattened him with a lightning right jab that left him lying straight in the street, then strode right on saying, "I'm tired of hearing that man talk. Anyway, the fat's in the fire now. He'll either shut up and leave us alone or come gunning."

As we mounted our horses, Jud Sykes looked out the saloon window, wiping blood from the corner of his mouth. Hate distorted his face as he watched us go.

#

Before leaving town, we stopped at Joe Warner's store. Beck pounded on the door until he roused the proprietor. John and Joe soon came out of the store and went around the back of the building to a separate shed several yards away. When they returned, Beck carried two parcels, each covered in burlap. He very carefully slipped one into each compartment of his saddlebags. His curious mission finished, we rode home on a moonlit trail.

Chapter 22

THE SUN JUST broke over the mountains as I walked out to do some chores. Beck was looking over the ruins of the barn, tossing aside blackened boards in preparation for rebuilding.

I watched him for a couple of minutes. "John?"

"Yeah?"

"You sure were something in that fight last night, the way you whipped all those men."

He looked over another board and threw it into a keeper pile. "You helped."

"Not all that much. I kept getting thrown out on my face, but you beat four of them."

"I guess it was a pretty good tussle at that. But you did keep that one feller off me for a time while I worked on the other three."

I smiled. "He did look pretty green around the gills after I kicked him."

Beck laughed. "That he did."

"How did you do it? Your fists flew like lightning bolts. Did you know you could win before you started?"

"I didn't. But I thought it was the best way to make a point and all of us get out of it alive." He heaved part of a burnt log into the discard pile. "First, a burnt barn isn't reason enough to kill men over."

I helped Beck throw out another log. "But there were four of them."

"Well, I figured the cards were in my favor. A lot of cowpunchers aren't that good with their fists. They think they have to do everything with a rope, a gun, or from the top of a saddle. Now, Irish track workers, they really know how to box."

"Where did you learn to box?"

"From Irish track workers." He grinned. "Also, I learned some techniques from Bat Masterson."

"Bat Masterson, the lawman?"

"The very same. He and I used to play cards together. He loved boxing. Called it the manly art of self-defense."

"Could you teach me?"

He looked me over and thought a moment. "It's a mean world sometimes. Could come in handy for a young man to understand the proper use of fisticuffs. Come down by the creek."

I followed, aware of the water gurgling behind me as I turned to face Beck in the clearing.

"Remember, to fight well you have to fight smart. The idea is to hit the other guy without him hitting you. Most fellas get mad and just start swinging. It helps to get mad yourself, but watch and think about what you're doing. Fight with a controlled anger. You've got to want to hit that man hard and fast. But don't go in flailing all over the place. Watch what he is doing and counter with blocks and ducks. Then see where he is unprotected and hit there. You ready?"

"Yeah." Excitement lurched within me.

"Now, keep your elbows down and you're fists up like this." He held his fists above his bent elbows. "That way it's hard for him to hit your face or belly."

"Okay."

"Hit me."

"Huh?"

"Hit me."

"But I might … *hit* you."

"If you do, it will be my fault."

I swung and Beck ducked, leaving me nothing but air.

"Again."

I swung again, but he blocked the punch and shot his right fist to within an inch of my face.

"See what I mean?"

"Uh huh."

We continued to spar for several minutes

"You're doing good, son. Now, faster."

As fast as I could think, I feinted with my left, and as Beck lifted his arms, I hit him in the stomach with my right, bringing a huff of air. I swung my left fist into his face. John reeled backward and glared at me.

For a breathless moment, I stepped back, fearing I just stepped into big trouble, but then Beck laughed. "That's it! Now you've got it."

"Hey, what are you two doing out there? Breakfast is getting cold." Jenny stood, watching us from the porch.

"We are just practicing the manly art of self-defense," I said. Beck and I laughed as we walked toward the cabin.

Beck looked up from his flapjacks. "Somebody's coming. Sounds like a wagon."

In a couple minutes, a knock sounded at the door. Jenny opened it. "Why, Mr. Warner. Nice to see you. Come in. Have some breakfast."

"Thanks. I ate before I left, but I'd thank ya' for a cup of that coffee I smell brewing."

"Come sit a spell, Joe." Beck pushed back a chair. "What brings you out this early?"

"Well, sir, I'm out passin' the word to the folks that don't git to town much, that there's gonna be a big barn dance out at the Logan ranch between here and Ridgeway come Saturday."

"Oh, that sounds exciting!" Jenny handed Joe a steaming cup.

"Thanks, Miss Foster." He took a sip of coffee. "Yep. It's gonna be a big shindig. Folks comin' from all over."

"Can we go?" Jenny looked at Beck and me. "We haven't had time to socialize and meet some of our neighbors."

"I guess we all could use a little fun for a change." Beck turned to me. "What's your thought, Mr. Foster?"

"It's just an old dance."

"There'll be lots of good food. And probably some pretty girls about your age." Joe Warner winked at me.

I blushed. "I can't dance."

"I'll teach you," Jenny offered.

"Well, what about it? Time comes when a man needs to learn some of the social graces, especially around the ladies." Beck leaned back in his chair.

"Oh, all right."

Jenny clapped her hands.

"I best be gittin' on." Joe rose from his chair. "I need to make a couple more stops to pass the word. Much obliged for that fine coffee,

Miss Foster. It tasted real good. Better even than I make myself."

"I learned from my mother." Jenny smiled.

"She taught you good, girl."

Joe moved to the door. "See you folks at the hoedown, the good Lord willin' and the creek don't rise."

#

I barely had my last bite of breakfast finished when Jenny took my hand and pulled me to the center of the room. "John, push the table and chairs back."

I pulled away. "What are you doing, Sis?"

"I'm going to teach you to dance."

"Now?"

"The sooner we start, the more time you'll have to learn."

"What if I mess it up?"

"Don't worry," Beck said. "Most fellas just stomp around to the music and have fun. Just try not to step on the lady's feet."

"This won't be as easy without music." Jenny thought for a minute. "John, do you know any square dance calls?"

"Yeah, I think I remember a couple." He placed one foot on a chair and clapped a rhythm. "Now, grab your partner and do-see-do ..."

I stumbled along, trying to follow Jenny through the steps. After a few minutes, she held out her hand to John. "Join us."

Beck whirled and stomped along with us until we nearly fell over each other and laughed until our sides hurt.

After a minute's rest, Jenny took my hand again. "Now, for a waltz. Put your other hand around my waist."

"Aw, do I have to?"

"No. You can just stand there looking silly all evening at the girl who wants to dance with you."

"What if no girls want to?"

"A tall, handsome hombre like you? The girls will be falling all over each other to be close to you," Beck said.

My face warmed again.

"I declare, you're as tall as your sister already."

I looked back at Jenny and realized I was looking eye to eye at her.

"Now follow my steps in a kind of a square." Jenny placed my hand around her waist and then took my other hand into hers.

After an awkward beginning, I finally got the hang of it. It wasn't too bad.

"When you dance with a girl, you count the steps in your head and lead her around in the direction you want to go."

"I don't know why people get all excited about this dancing business."

Beck chuckled. "The first time you move around a dance floor with a pretty gal in your arms, you'll understand."

Chapter 23

THE LOGAN RANCH was huge, about 60,000 acres, with a steer for every two acres. I gazed up from our wagon at the two-story log home. Sitting in a pine grove on the top of a hill, it stood out in vivid contrast against the San Juan Mountains bathed in late afternoon sunlight.

A whole steer roasted on a large spit in the yard. One servant basted the beef as another turned the spit.

A man as tall and husky as Beck greeted us while one of the hands took care of our horses and wagon. "Howdy, folks. I'm Jim Logan, and this is my wife, Molly." He nodded to a short, red-haired woman at his side.

"It is so good of you to come." Her words carried a British accent.

"Thank you for your kind invitation." Jenny gave a small curtsey, something I had never seen her do before. "I'm Jenny Foster. This is my brother, David, and this is our friend Mr. John Beck."

"And this is our daughter, Sarah." Mrs. Logan looked at a girl about my age with red flowing hair like her mother. The prettiest girl I ever saw. Excitement rose in my chest.

"How do you do?" A hint of her mother's accent colored her voice.

"M-miss." I tipped my hat.

We shook hands all around. Mrs. Logan and Sarah invited Jenny into the house to freshen up while the men talked of land and livestock prices. Soon more people arrived, and Logan offered more greetings and introductions.

Dinner, served on long tables outside, smelled sumptuous. There was beef, beans, and an assortment of dishes supplied by the lady guests, including fried chicken, noodles, and a variety of cakes and fruit pies. My mouth watered above my growling stomach.

Mr. Logan stood at the end of one of the tables. "Folks, if you'll care to join us, I asked Reverend Holloway to say grace."

All became quiet as a stocky, middle-aged preacher began. "Lord, we thank you for the abundance that we share today which Your hand has provided. Father, we have all come to this magnificent land of Your mighty creation and built our homes and ranches by the sweat of our brow as is directed in Your enduring word. Make us good stewards of Your gifts, good neighbors, and worthy servants, sharing Your love and peace and the hope of Your eternal salvation with all we meet. In Jesus' precious name. Amen."

After the minister finished, I noticed Frank Maxwell sitting at one of the tables. I hoped the words of the prayer sank into him.

As the sun set with an ember-like glow behind the mountains, someone lit lanterns inside the barn, emptied and cleaned for the festivities. The fragrance of fresh hay permeated the space. A band warmed up at one end. About twenty couples, some with children, moved onto the dance floor or sat on bales of straw around the perimeter.

Maxwell talked to Logan over by the table that held coffee, punch, lemonade, and more desserts. Maxwell then stepped over to a blond-haired boy about my age, whispered something to him, and nodded toward me. The boy eyed me over his glass of punch and disappeared into the crowd.

"Oh, that poor Boggard boy." A woman near me shook her head while staring in the direction the blond fella had disappeared.

"Poor? Erma, he's a hooligan," the woman beside her scolded. "Ain't nothing poor about that child. He's a blight on our town."

The first woman scowled. "Now let's not be uncharitable, Mae. You know he comes from a bad home."

They moved off as the band fired up with a lively square dance tune. I went to the table and picked up a bottle of sarsaparilla. Beck came up, speaking to the fellow dipping punch out of an elegant crystal bowl. "Has this stuff got a kick to it?"

"Nope." The fellow stopped in mid-dip. "The Logans are Christians and teetotalers. But a couple cowhands might have a bottle to pass around out back."

Beck took a deep breath. "Well, I do feel the need for a breath of fresh air." He grinned. "Excuse me, gentlemen." He disappeared out the back door.

Something bumped my shoulder, jarring some of my drink onto

the floor.

"Hey watch where you're goin', clumsy."

When I turned, the blond boy glared at me. I looked at the boy who stood taller than me by a good three inches.

"I wasn't moving, so it seems you're the clumsy one."

"You calling me a liar? I'm Tim Boggard, and nobody calls me that."

I opened my mouth to tell him what I thought but remembered what Beck told me about fighting only for what's important—even to walk away and let people think what they will.

"You lookin' for a fight?" He doubled his fists.

"No. It's just a little misunderstanding."

"You pushed me, boy. You better apologize or be ready to go settle this outside."

My nerves fired like Fourth-of-July rockets, but I took a deep breath and gave him my biggest smile. "Well then, I apologize. No hard feelings." I picked up a glass of punch and put it into his hand. "You have a nice evening." I noticed the look of surprised confusion on the young fellow's face as I walked away. I just hoped he didn't see me shaking.

Beck came back in with another rancher, a short man who wore a full beard. He spoke in a confidential tone. "Maxwell's pushin' me hard to get out. My ranch ain't that big. I only got a couple hired hands. We aren't gunmen."

"Anybody else having trouble?"

"Yeah. Three other small ranches, all near Maxwell's spread. The same story. Get out or get hurt. Some others have done got out already. I heard you're experienced with a gun, Beck. I was thinkin' maybe if we all band together with you leading us, we could buffalo Maxwell out of his game."

Beck looked straight at the fellow. "Problem is, when he makes his move, he'll hit us one at a time. We're too far apart to ride for help or to get to each other in time."

"I got family, and I ain't gonna take on an army of gunmen if I don't see no chance in it."

Beck hooked his thumbs in his belt and thought a moment. "Pass the word around to the other landowners, and let's all meet at Foster's place Friday evening. We'll put our heads together to see what we can come up with. Maybe we can avoid gunplay."

"Thanks, Beck. We'll be there." The man turned and walked outside.

Beck turned to me. "Is that all right with you, Dave? You and your sister are the owners. This is not really my decision to make."

"Sure. I'm agreeable to working with my neighbors."

"Looks like Maxwell thinks he's gonna be the big bug around here. One thing for sure … when the action starts, it will happen fast."

"John, you need to dance." Jenny held out her arms as she approached.

Beck made an exaggerated bow. "Miss Foster, I would be honored to take you up on that offer." The two moved easily about the floor. Jenny's eyes glowed as she smiled up at him.

Before the dance ended, Luke Dawson came up and tapped Beck on the shoulder to cut in. I thought it was a dumb custom, but apparently, it was acceptable in polite dancing.

Beck looked at the young man who was nearly as tall as him, then turned back to Jenny. She nodded, and Luke whisked her away as Beck watched them. In a minute, he stepped over to me. "Help me keep an eye on that fella. He seems like he might be all right, but working for Maxwell, I don't know if we can trust him."

Later, they all joined in a square dance, circling around and laughing. Beck partnered with a plump lady about his age.

I now held a glass of punch, feeling awkward with nothing else to do. But then I noticed Sarah Logan standing against the opposite wall with another girl. Sarah turned and looked in my direction.

My stomach jumped around inside me. I fidgeted with my drink. She sure was the prettiest thing I ever saw.

"It's time you stopped standing and started dancing." Beck spoke from behind me.

My heartbeat picked up tempo.

"I think that little gal is waiting for you."

Now my stomach churned as if full-sized buzzards flapped around in it. I wanted to be close to that girl more than anything, if I didn't pass out first. Strange, I never felt scared around girls back in school.

I set the cup on the table and shuffled forward as if in a dream. When I got to her, I couldn't think of a thing to say. She smiled, glanced down at the floor, then said, "Good evening, Mr. Foster."

Mister Foster. I declare, I grew six inches that moment. "Good evening, Miss Logan." The other girl giggled.

"Well, miss … I was wondering if … you know … if you'd like to …"

"Dance?"

"Yeah."

"Yes. Thank you, sir." The slight British lilt to her words was like music.

Sarah led me to the center of the floor. Her hand was flower-petal soft. The green plaid dress she wore made a swishing sound with each step. When she held out her arms, I moved into them and slipped my other hand around her waist.

The feel of her body moving beneath my arm sent my heart drumming till I thought it would burst. She moved left, and I moved right, barely missing her foot. It caused us both to stumble.

"I'm sorry, miss. I'm real new at this dancing business."

Sarah chuckled. "It's all right. I'm still learning myself. You just lead, and I'll try to follow."

We moved together, and for several minutes, waves of new feelings I'd never experienced before washed over me.

Something thumped my shoulder. "Hey, I'm cutting in."

It was Tim Boggard. I wanted to tell him to go stick his head in a pickle barrel but glanced at Sarah. She nodded.

"I'll save the last dance for you, Mister Foster." Her voice was so soft it was like a warm spring breeze to my ear.

I moved back to the wall and watched them with gritted teeth. It was bad enough that Blondie was dancing with the girl, but he danced well.

He moved her toward the open back door. He said something to her then bowed gallantly. In a moment, they disappeared into the dark.

I began to pace. They only stepped out for some fresh air. That wasn't so unusual. Was it? But what if he wasn't a gentleman? It grew warm in the barn. *Real warm.* I could use some air myself. I stomped toward the door.

As I was about to step outside, Miss Logan came marching back in, Blondie following right behind her. "Come on. Just one." He grabbed her arm.

"No! I'd rather kiss a horse." Sarah jerked her arm free and continued on.

Tim Boggard followed, but I stepped between them. "Leave Miss Logan alone. She doesn't want your company. And a real man always respects a lady's wishes." Beck's words echoed in my head.

Boggard's eyebrows arched. "Oh? So chicken boy is playing the banty rooster. You gonna fight me now?"

I shook again but with rage. I wanted nothing more than to knock that arrogant grin off his face. "No. But if you bother the young lady once more, I will beat you into the dirt."

I turned to find the girl who stirred me so, but a strong hand spun me around. A fist smashed my face with dizzying pain. I pushed myself up from the dirt, barely aware of how I got there.

"You're not running away this time, boy. Come on and fight."

I stood, dusting myself off. "All right. You started it. I'll finish it." I doubled my fists and moved into the fighting stance Beck showed me.

Boggard grinned wider. "I'm sure gonna enjoy this." He rushed me, arms swinging. I ducked and left him with nothing but air, and Boggard turned in confusion.

He swung a second time, and again, I ducked.

"Stand still and fight, you little brat. Fight like a …"

I launched three left jabs. Boggard's head bobbed back, and I followed with a right hook. He staggered.

Blondie shook it off and came at me, bellowing like a bull.

Stepping aside, I shoved him sprawling into the dust. I ached to flail away at him, but Beck's words rang in my head. 'Fight with controlled anger. Keep your wits about you.'

Boggard jumped up, charging in with a roundhouse punch. I stepped into it, blocking his blow, then drove my right fist into his stomach. I threw a left hook and finished with the hardest right hook I could muster. Tim landed on his back with a puff of dust.

Someone stepped in to stop the fight, but a voice rose over the din. "Nah, let 'em finish it."

I waited, breathing hard. The boy struggled to a sitting position. "Boggard, you want to call it good, or do you want to go on?"

"Naw." He raised one hand and rubbed his jaw with the other. "I'm done."

I walked away, barely noticing the chuckles of the collected onlookers.

Beck stopped me at the door, grabbed my face, and turned my cheek up to his view. "Yep, you're gonna have a real good shiner there."

Out of the corner of my eye, I noticed Mr. Logan escorting Tim Boggard out the front doors by his shirt collar.

"Well, sir," Beck said, "you've had quite a night. Had a good meal, danced with a pretty girl, and defended a lady's honor. You deserve a drink." He handed me a bottle of sarsaparilla. I held its coolness against my aching cheek

Jenny ran in with two other ladies from the area where the beef was being roasted. "Your face! What happened?"

"He's fine. Just fine," Beck said. He slapped me on the back so hard that I choked on my drink. "Now I think it's time to say goodnight to our hosts."

We met the Logans on the way out. "Thank you folks for a fine shindig." Beck shook Logan's hand.

"I'm glad you enjoyed it." Mr. Logan turned to me. "Young man, Sarah told us what you did for her. We're obliged."

"You're welcome, sir."

"Beck, you're raising a real gentleman here."

"Yep, he'll be a man to ride the river with."

My sister grinned at our hosts. "Mrs. Logan, thank you for your hospitality. We'd be proud to return your kindness by having you folks over for dinner sometime." Jenny blushed. "But it won't be as fancy as all this."

Mrs. Logan took Jenny's hands. "We would be delighted to come."

Mr. Logan turned to me again. "I think Sarah has something to say to you, David."

Her cheeks changed to a rosy pink. "Thank you, David ... ah, Mr. Foster. You are very brave."

"It wasn't all that much. But I couldn't let anybody treat you disrespectful." My own cheeks warmed. The only ones *not* blushing were the older men.

We all finished our goodbyes and took our leave. The horses were all ready to go. I was about to step up into the wagon when light footsteps ran up behind me, and the Logans' daughter appeared next to me. Without a word, she kissed me on the cheek and ran back to the house.

I climbed into the back of our wagon, a silly grin growing on my burning face as Jenny and John chuckled.

Once seated, Beck said, "Yep, quite a night." He flicked the reins, and we headed for home.

#

Upon arriving at our cabin, exhausted but happy, we went to bed right away. Beck disappeared into his room first. The lantern near the door lit our way. "I'll get the light," Jenny said.

As I walked up the stairs, she touched Beck's jacket where it hung upon a wall peg, stroking her fingers through the fringes. She blew out the light and crossed in the dark to her room.

Chapter 24

THE MORNING DAWNED sunny and warm. Jenny had opened the windows already.

"Where's John?" I yawned as I sat at the table.

"I don't know." Jenny didn't look up from the eggs she was frying. "I heard him leave before daylight. Hunting maybe. Or sometimes I think he goes off into the woods to be alone. A few times I've even seen him, in the evening, standing up on the hill by Papa's grave."

I stepped to the stove and poured a cup of coffee. Jenny turned, looking straight at me. "You'll be as tall as Papa before long."

"Can't call me 'little brother' anymore."

She shook her head as I sat at the table. "Oh, by the way, *little brother*, when I gathered the eggs, I noticed that something has been trying to dig under the chicken coop."

"Probably a fox. I'll get the shotgun after breakfast. Check for tracks. Maybe I'll get lucky and find its den." I ate fast, eager to get to the hunt.

Breakfast over, I picked up the shotgun from the gun rack above the fireplace and stepped out onto the porch. My heart near stopped when I found myself facing three mounted men. The one in the middle was Jud Sykes.

"Howdy, boy. Is yer sister at home? I come a-courting." As proof Sykes held up a weedy looking bouquet. "You just go on in and tell her I'm here."

"What's the matter, you can't talk to a lady without bringing friends to help you?" I nodded toward the other men.

"These fellers just came along for the ride. Thought you might have some coffee to share."

"You best move along. Beck will be back any minute. He won't like you here." I hoped no one heard my voice quiver.

"Naw, we watched him ride out a little while ago. Appeared to be headed toward your south range."

My heart raced like a mustang running from a pack of wolves, death at its heels. I threw up a silent prayer. *Oh Lord, help me. What do I do now? What would Beck do?*

Sykes moved as if to dismount.

"Don't get off that horse." I lifted the shotgun and aimed it at the man's chest.

Sykes halted, looking at the double barrels pointing at him. I pulled back the first hammer, the click sharp in the clear morning air. The man eased back into his saddle.

"When a man comes to call at somebody's ranch, he waits until he's invited to dismount. You weren't invited."

"Boy, you're the one bein' impolite. And me here just to make a social call. Now, why is that?"

"It's because I don't like you."

Sykes' face turned mean. "And I don't like a half-growed kid pointing a gun at me. You put that thing down, or I'll take it away from you and smash your head in with it."

"You'll die trying." I held the gun steady.

"Don't be stupid, boy. There's three of us, and you only got two shots. You pull a trigger and you're dead."

"Probably so, but that won't make any difference to you."

"Yeah, why?"

"Because you'll already be dead."

Sykes hesitated.

"No matter how it starts, any man goes for a gun, flinches, or blinks an eye, I'm going to kill you first."

Sykes sat very still. Uncertainty mixed with his usually arrogant expression.

"I figure I'll kill one more man as I go down." I clicked back the second hammer. "There's one thing certain. You're going to die today. The only question is which one of these men loves you enough to die with you."

Sykes licked his lips as he turned to his partners, neither of whom returned his look. One seemed to be interested in things on the ground or in the sky and such. One stared toward the cabin.

Jud Sykes glared at me. I kept the shotgun on him, but my arm grew tired. I didn't know how much longer I could hold up the heavy weapon.

"Come on, fellers. Let's go for now." Jud looked back at me. "This ain't over, boy. I'll be back."

"Then look at the ground around you."

He looked down with curiosity, then back up at me.

"If you come back, this will be the spot where you'll die."

The man and his companions turned their horses and rode slowly away. I watched them until they crossed the creek. As I turned to enter the cabin, I noticed a rifle protruding from the window.

I leaned against the doorpost. Jenny laid down her rifle and ran to me. "You were so brave out there." She hugged me, stepped back, and looked into my face. "Are you all right?"

"I think I'm going to be sick," I rasped.

Chapter 25

MORNING BROKE CRISP and bright, scents of grass and pine drifting along with bird songs on a gentle breeze. The fragrance of fresh-brewed coffee wafted into my room from the kitchen.

It was all shattered by a gunshot. I jumped out of bed and ran, still in my longjohns, to the front door, grabbing a rifle from its wall peg as I went. Beck already stood on the porch with his pistol drawn.

We watched the direction from where the sound had come. After a tense moment, Jenny stepped from behind the chicken coop. She held up a dead fox by the tail in one hand and her rifle in the other. "That's one varmint that won't be eating my chickens." She inspected the thing more closely. "When I get it skinned and cured, it should make a fine muff for next winter."

Beck laughed. "Yep, girl, you're becoming a real pioneer woman."

Jenny smiled.

Beck turned to me as we went back inside. "Your sister will make some rancher a first-class wife someday. He better be a good man, though, or I declare, she'll toss him out and run the ranch all on her own."

"She practically runs this one now," I said.

Beck laughed again.

#

An atmosphere of solemnity pervaded the room like the quiet heaviness before a tornado. Jenny refilled coffee cups for the men seated around our table under the yellow light of the lantern.

"My wife had a garden until Maxwell's men trampled it one night.

Another night they burned my barn," said Jake Wilson, a short, wiry man with a beard. I recognized him as the one who had spoken to Beck at the Logans' party.

"Well, somebody shot my best ranch hand while he was out checking fences," added Tom Smith as he ran his fingers through his red hair. "Then two of my other hands up and quit."

Silas Jackson, a tall thin fellow, sat in his chair and said nothing, just listened.

Wilson put down his cup. "We've got to do something. We're all small ranchers. We don't have the gunmen to face that army of Maxwell's. What do you think, Beck?"

Beck took another sip of his coffee before speaking. "If we could get rid of Maxwell, the rest will take everything they can carry from his place and move on. They haven't got the brains or ambition to run a ranch. Actually, there's no professional gun hands among them except for Sykes. They're just hired toughs. The thing is, we've got to do it legal. I'd hoped to find a wanted poster on Maxwell, but he seems to be keeping out of sight of the law so far."

"What about getting a federal marshal involved?" asked Wilson.

"We could, but that would take time. Then he'd have to investigate the evidence which Maxwell has been right careful to hide. So, it's our word against his."

"How about us all goin' over together to his place and shoot it out?" Smith said.

"Now you're talking about a fullscale range war." Beck put his cup down. "A lot of men on both sides will get killed."

"So, now what?" Jackson shrugged.

"One man could ride into Goldstrike and send a letter for a marshal. Maybe, in the meantime, we could corral one of Maxwell's men and get him to talk."

"Or we could git killed before any law has time to git here. And I ain't goin' to ride nowhere to send a letter and git bushwhacked," said Smith. He paused. "Beck, we know you got a reputation with a gun. Maybe you could just wait along a trail and bushwhack Maxwell."

"No." Beck lifted his cup to his lips.

Smith persisted. "But it'd be easy for you."

"No!" Beck slammed his cup down on the table.

There was a long silence until Smith stood. "This ain't gittin' us nowhere. I'm done. I'm pullin' up stakes and movin' on." He started toward the door.

"Hold on, Tom, I'll ride a ways with you," said Jackson as he stood. He turned to Jenny. "Thanks for the coffee, Miss Foster."

She nodded. "You're welcome."

Jake shrugged."Tom, Silas, let's think on Beck's idea a spell and get back together in a couple days." The others nodded as they left. Wilson turned back to us. "That all right with you, Mr. Beck?"

"Yeah, fine."

"Good night." Wilson started out the door, then stopped. Looking straight at Beck, he said, "I never expected to see my neighbors lose their nerve. I don't know if I can convince them to come back and talk about taking a stand again or not. I'll try, but Maxwell seems to be holding all the cards. I know one thing, though. If he gets past you, the others will clear out, and I won't be able to protect my place. I'll have to leave, too." He closed the door quietly as he stepped out.

After the men left, Jenny approached Beck. "What do you think about this meeting, John?"

"I think we are going to be facing Maxwell and his men by ourselves." He got up and went to his room.

#

Beck stepped out right after breakfast, and soon the sound of pounding came to our ears. Jenny and I went to see what Beck was up to in the new, nearly completed barn. Four wooden boxes occupied the table, the last of which he'd just finished hammering together. Next to those boxes sat several packages of bullets and two small stacks of slender red cylinders.

"That's dynamite!" Jenny exclaimed.

"Smart girl. Figured that out right off, did you?" Beck lifted the last box for inspection.

"What in the world are you planning to do with this?" Jenny asked.

"When you told me about Maxwell's men coming here the other day while I was away, I knew things are just gonna get worse. If he takes this ranch, the other ranchers will fold. Now that Maxwell knows he can't scare us or burn us out, he'll have to drive as out … or kill us. When he tries, we'll have some surprises for him. Greatest thing in a fight is surprise. I remember one time when I was just a kid in the army, Confederate that is, a few of us scattered a whole Yankee platoon. We slipped in close when they weren't expecting us and rode through them, shooting and yelling like a hundred Injuns. The Yanks had us outnumbered two to one, but they flew off like the whole Confederate army was after 'em." Beck laughed.

"You don't think we've persuaded Mr. Maxwell to leave us alone?" Jenny's brows knitted in a frown.

"I doubt it."

"I guess I never really believed it would come to this," Jenny said. "It all seemed like a game somehow. Maxwell made a move. We made a countermove. It always worked out. But, now we may have to kill to keep our home, or … we could be killed."

Beck turned from the table and looked at us. "That's the way it's likely to be. Maybe you two better have a conference and decide for sure what you want to do. If you stay, you'll probably have to fight—and kill—to keep your home. If you've got doubts when the fight starts, you'll die here. Know this: Maxwell will kill you to get this land. It won't bother his conscience a bit. You all decide right now. If you stay, I'll help you. If you pack up and leave, you'll be safe. Then I reckon I'll just ride out and go on about my business. I won't have to bother with this stuff anymore, either." Beck nodded toward the dynamite.

"I don't know. I'm confused. Everything is happening so fast now. I don't want any more killing here." Jenny rubbed her temple. "But we've worked so hard. We've come through so much. I don't want to give it up to a thief and murderer."

"What's wrong with a person defending his property and his life?" I demanded. "Our father was killed here. That was wrong. We've been threatened. Our barn was burned, and that was wrong. I'm not going to run, or stand back, or step aside. I don't care what anybody else does. On this land or under it, I'm staying. And nobody, *nobody*, is going to change that."

The other two stared at me in silence. In that moment, a fire and strength burned from within that caught me by surprise, almost like I stood in my place as a man beside my father and John Beck.

Beck broke the silence. "You'd both be safer to leave. I don't like the idea of either of you getting hurt, but it's something both of you should decide. Not just you, Dave, or me. So we better hear Jenny's decision, too."

As we looked toward Jenny, she lowered her head as in thought, rubbed her hand back and forth on the table but remained silent.

Beck continued. "The question that bothers me, though, is what you'll do if you leave. The likes of Maxwell, in some degree or another, lives everywhere in the world. What happens the next time somebody wants you to run away?" He tapped the table. "In some way, a person's always fighting or running whether it's running from somebody else or yourself or some evil. Or you might fight from a stockade, a cornfield being eaten by critters, or fight evil from a pulpit. But every person born, each in his own way, runs from or stands up to what's threatening their way of life."

Beck paused, rubbing the tip of his mustache. "If it was only me, I'd stay and wouldn't give those rats an inch. But this is not about me. It's about the two of you. The West is changing. Men like Maxwell and me are getting fewer. I won't hold it against you if you decide not to kill or die over a patch of dirt. There's no shame in taking the way of peace. As a matter of fact, I would feel a lot better if you choose the safer route."

Jenny remained silent a moment longer. She turned and looked out the back window where she could see our father's grave on the hill. Then, gazing out the door as if looking far into the future, she said, "I'll stay."

"Realize this is a life and death decision. Are you both sure this is what you want to do?" Beck looked intently at us.

For the first time, a twinge of fear over our situation pricked my heart. Yet, I didn't want Beck to leave us, and I didn't want to leave what had become our home. Especially to someone who didn't deserve it. Also, down deep, I believed that John Beck was indestructible, and with him leading us, we could conquer all the dangers the world would ever throw at us. "I vote to stay."

Jenny nodded.

Beck stared at us with a sad expression. I would not understand the reason for that expression until those days of innocence and blood passed.

"Guess that's it," Beck said. "We've got work to do. Dave, get a couple shovels and everybody follow me." He led us to a spot between the house and the creek bank. There he directed Jenny and me to dig two small holes about fourteen feet apart. He then carefully placed some dynamite sticks into each box and placed them in the holes so half of each box showed above ground. Finally, he covered the boxes with just enough dirt so they were hidden from view from the direction of the creek.

"Now, these boxes will keep the dew off the dynamite until it's needed," Beck said. "If Maxwell's men come charging straight in, we'll fire into these mounds and cut down the odds or at least cause some fine confusion. The attackers won't have much cover to get close. The few trees near the house aren't big enough for good concealment. The only way they could get close without being under our guns is to slip in behind the outhouse, and that can be taken care of by fixing up the rest of the dynamite at the corner."

Beck was fired with action and plans, fully absorbed in that destructiveness that had so much been a part of his past. A chilling discomfort overcame me from it. As he went around the house to plant more of his deadly seeds, he turned back to us and said, "By the way, if either of you need to go to the outhouse … sit light."

Chapter 26

LATER THAT MORNING, I found Beck in the barn again, checking and cleaning the rifles. "I'm going to ride out and scout around in a little while," he said. "The only way Maxwell's men could have known that we were away from the cabin was if somebody watched us. While I'm gone, you and your sister stay close to the house. By the way, where is Jenny?"

"She went somewhere down the creek to take a bath, I think."

No sooner had I said it than Jenny screamed somewhere outside. Beck sprang from the workbench, running, rifle in hand, toward the creek. I followed close behind him.

In a few seconds, we found her hiding among some leafy tree branches that hung low over the water. She stood waist deep in the water, back to us, covering her front with her arms. "A man! There's a man watching me on the other side of the creek." She nodded toward the far bank. "Up there by that big log." Looking back over her shoulder at us, her eyes went wide, and she ducked under the water. Seconds later, she emerged only far enough that her head and tops of her shoulders broke the surface.

"The two of you stay hidden, and don't move." Beck took a position behind a large tree where he could watch the forest beyond the creek. The opposite bank was high with a steep slope, covered with brush and trees. A man jumped from behind a bush and made a mad scramble for the denser woods. Beck fired. A wild yelp accompanied the roar of the rifle. At the moment of impact, the wounded man leaped and disappeared over the top of the slope.

"Cover me." Beck threw his rifle to me and waded into the creek. He held his pistol shoulder high to keep it dry and ready for another shot. I kept the rifle trained on the far shore until Beck crossed. Then, I followed.

Once on the other side, I saw no sign of Beck, so skilled was he in moving secretively through the forest. I found him in a clearing, standing over the spy. The man was lying on the ground, holding his bleeding thigh. His face distorted with pain and fear as he squawked, "Don't kill me. I didn't do nothing! You near ruint m' leg. It hurts terrible. I need a doctor."

"It won't hurt long," Beck said through clenched teeth." I'm going to put you out of your misery right now unless you tell me everything I want to know."

"I don't know nothing. I wuz just minding m' own business, doin' some hunting when somebody screamed, an' afore I knowed it, everybody's shooting at me."

"You were sent here to watch us, maybe even work in some bushwhacking, and if you lie to me again, it'll be the last words you ever speak." Beck cocked the pistol.

"No, no! I wuz just supposed to watch, not hurt nobody. A man's only human, you know. I happened to see the lady in the water an' thought I'd watch a spell, but I didn't mean no harm, honest!"

"Who you working for?"

"Frank Maxwell."

"Are you the one who shot Jim Foster in the back?"

"No."

"Who did?"

"I can't say."

Beck's pistol roared, and the ground next to the outlaw's head exploded in a cloud of dust and black smoke.

"Jud! Jud Sykes. Maxwell said that wuz his job. I had nothing to do with it, I swear!"

Beck holstered his pistol, grabbed the man by his shirt collar and belt, hoisted him to his feet, and rushed him to the place where the outlaw's horse was tied. All the while the man groaned and gasped, clutching his wound. "Oh, easy now. Ow! Easy, easy!"

Beck heaved him on his horse and led the animal toward the creek. "Mister, you're gonna stay and visit a spell … tell your story to some neighbors of mine and to a marshal."

The man on the horse went wide eyed. "No! Maxwell will kill me. Besides, he's still gonna come after you, no matter what."

"I'll see that he won't get far if he does come after us."

"All right, I'll go with you," the man said. Then, without warning, he slapped his horse with his spurs, even with his bad leg. He yanked the reins out of Beck's hand and jerked them hard to the right. In the excitement, the frightened horse reared and threw off its rider.

We approached the fallen man. Blood spattered on a rock beneath his head. Beck listened to the fellow's chest for a heartbeat, shook his head, and cursed under his breath.

I didn't try to correct his language. My heart sank with dread.

"Well, that does it," Beck said. "It's all coming to a head now."

"I want the first shot at Jud Sykes," I declared.

"If I don't see him first," Beck said.

Chapter 27

A TIME OF waiting and preparation followed the incident with the spy. Beck rode into the forest twice a day for the next two days and disappeared nightly for an hour or more. He was more alert than ever before. As we worked rebuilding the barn, he constantly scanned the ridge and forest with those hawk-like eyes. When eating in the house, he sat facing the door. At night, we tightly bolted the door and windows. He spent the next night hidden on the mountain away from the house, keeping watch.

"The fat's in the fire," Beck said after breakfast as he gathered us behind the house for target practice. "Frank Maxwell can't let us live here now that we know he had your pa killed. Even if that man of his didn't go back to him, he'll start adding things up. Anyway, there's been gunplay now, and there's no turning back."

For an hour, Jenny and I fired the rifles and Pa's pistol at pinecones and empty bottles. We learned to reload fast enough that we could keep up a steady fire. Meanwhile, Beck watched and directed our progress, urging Jenny to raise the elevation of the rifle barrel to compensate for the distance, or telling me to allow for the wind, and, "Squeeze, don't jerk the trigger."

Beck pulled me aside. "You're making progress with that pistol, but if it comes to a shootout between you and Jud Sykes, don't try to outdraw him. He fancies himself as a gun hand, but he's far from the best. He is good enough, though, that you wouldn't have a chance. Your pa's pistol and holster are not designed for speed, anyway. Move too fast and your gun may hang up in the holster or go off in the dirt at your feet. Figure out something that gives you an edge if it comes to that. I'll try to get to him first, but we've got to plan for the unexpected in a gun battle."

Finally, Beck ended the practice with a demonstration of shooting from a galloping horse. He rode at an angle to a small pine stump, firing as he rode. He guided the horse with his legs, leaving the reins draped over the pommel of the saddle, thus freeing his hands for aiming his weapon. The stump shattered, and splinters flew as he fired.

The performance was impressive, but Beck huffed when he missed his sixth shot. "I routed a half dozen hostile Apaches that way once. If I had shot like this, I might not be telling about it now. Surprise and speed can cut down the odds when you're outnumbered. Remember that. It may come in handy when Mr. Frank Maxwell comes calling."

"Don't you mean *if* he comes?" Jenny said.

"*When* he comes," Beck replied. "As a matter of fact, I might just sneak over to his place tonight and see if I can find out what he's cooking up."

#

Beck didn't have to go on his scouting mission. Late in the afternoon, a lone rider appeared on the ridge. As the stranger rode closer, there was nothing suspicious about his appearance. Yet that same cold chill that came over me the day Frank Maxwell came alone to see if we'd died during the winter swept down my spine.

The man rode with a relaxed, almost lazy manner as he eased the horse through the creek. He wore a long, black coat. A bowler hat sat cocked at a slant on his head above an ordinary face adorned only with a thin mustache and goatee. Overall, he had the appearance of a townsman, possibly a gambler or an undertaker.

I finally realized what disturbed me about the stranger. He had that same watchful look of a hunting wolf as John Beck.

"Jenny, Dave, git in the house." Beck's voice was low and firm.

"Howdy, folks," The rider tipped his hat toward the window where I suspected Jenny watched. He also nodded to me where I stood in the doorway, holding Pa's rifle.

"Stay on your horse and state yer business, Fallon." Beck leaned against the porch post, but his right hand hung near his pistol.

"Now, Beck, is that any way to greet an old friend after all these years?"

"You're not my friend. Now state your business and move on."

"Well, it ain't a social call, no how. I reckon you already guessed that I'm working for Frank Maxwell. As a negotiator, you might say. You know, John, it's getting harder for men in our business, law dogs an' courthouses springing up all over the place. We ain't getting any younger either. There's no need for killing in this situation. You come into town tomorrow morning, an' we can work something out. What do you say?"

"Tell Maxwell I'll come in and do my business directly with him. Don't try to stand in my way. You'll die if you do."

"Tomorrow then, about ten o'clock?"

"I'll be there."

"Getting warm today." Fallon removed his coat with deliberate slowness, laying it across the back of his saddle. The act revealed two pearl-handled pistols, one on each hip. Several notches marked the handles.

Beck and Fallon stared at each other for several seconds. My stomach churned as I tightened the grip on my rifle.

Fallon grinned, turned his horse, and rode away.

"Let's take a walk along the creek," Beck said to me.

I followed without a word until we were well away from the cabin. "Who was that?"

"His name's Ezekiel Fallon, a hired gun. One of the best ... and worst of his kind. Yes, sir, Zeke's got a name right out of the Bible, but it's the wrong name."

"There's not really going to be any negotiation tomorrow, is there?"

"No."

"Will he be alone?"

"Probably not."

"I'm going with you."

"No. Fallon is good, real good, but I think I can take him. I'll try to kill Maxwell and Sykes, too. If I do, your problems are over. If I don't, Frank Maxwell and his men, what's left of 'em, will come here. Jenny will need you then. If it comes to that, and if he's still alive, try to hit Sykes early in the fight. I've known a lot of bad men who'd still treat a woman decent. Jud won't. You understand what I'm saying?"

I nodded.

"Then try to git a clear shot at Maxwell, though he may stay toward the back of the fight."

We both fell silent for a minute.

"I want you to think hard on what I say next." Beck looked straight at me. "You've got Jenny to take care of. You voted to stay, but a shootout between just the two of you and a dozen hard cases will probably end in both of you being killed. In the morning, after I'm gone, you saddle and pack your horses. If I'm not back here by noon, put Jenny on a horse, tie her if you have to, and get out of here. Take the back trail to Ridgeway. You've got enough money to get you both back East. If you're gone when he gets here, there's a chance Maxwell won't follow."

John Beck's words stopped me. The possibility of him actually being killed had never really struck me before. "No!" I blurted out. "You can't talk that way. Nobody can beat you. You're the best shot and the toughest man there is. You're the best!"

He looked at me a long time before he spoke. His voice was firm. "I've told you that you gotta face facts the way they are. Every man that uses a gun knows that there's somebody somewhere who's better. I've lived by the gun most of my life, and someday, maybe tomorrow, it's the way I'll die. I have to face that possibility every day, and now you have to face it, too. That's the way it is."

The lump in my throat grew too big for me to speak, so I turned and walked back to my room in the loft. There, I struggled between my desire to be the man Beck wanted me to be and the urge to rush to him—to beg him to stay and run away with us from a world that had turned dark and frightening.

Sunset's orange rays painting the evening sky shook me from my thoughts. I had to see Beck. I had to stay close to him tonight because tomorrow ... "Jenny, where's John?" I demanded as I rushed through the house.

"Up on the hill."

He stood alone before my father's gravestone. John Beck was a dark shadow, silhouetted against a fire-red sky. He had laid his hat on a rock and appeared to be deep thought. With his thumbs hooked in his belt, John stood absolutely still, the breeze rustling his hair and the long fringes of his jacket.

I couldn't bring myself to break his meditation, so I stepped back into the trees just out of sight. In a minute, someone approached. It was Jenny. She stepped close to Beck but did not speak. He still looked at the rude cross marker as he said, "Your pa wanted me to look after you. I'm afraid now I'm not doing very well."

"I believe Papa would be grateful for all that you've done for us. I know I am." Jenny's voice was soft in the stillness of the twilight. There was a long pause. "I've been thinking about everything. Fallon is very good with a gun, isn't he? Better than any of Maxwell's men?"

"He's fair-to-middlin', I'd say."

"You may die."

"I reckon dying ain't so bad if it's for something or someone more important than yourself."

"John, I don't want the ranch if it means you'll be killed."

"I don't ever remember saying Fallon could beat me. Besides, there's something else I want you to think about." Beck turned to her. "In this last year, for the first time in a long time, I've been alive—really alive. You and Dave gave me that. Now, I'm going to give you this land. It's the only thing I can give you in the only way I know how. Don't ask me to stop before it's finished."

"All I know is that I don't want you to die. Please stay with us," Don't go to town tomorrow."

Silence.

"John, I love you!"

Now both were silent, avoiding each other's eyes. Finally, Jenny began again. "I've been afraid to say that because you might think it was just a young girl's foolish whim. But I am a woman, and I know how I feel. And I know that I love you."

Beck let out a long breath. "No, I don't think it's foolish ... because I've felt the same way about you for some time now."

Jenny looked back up at him as he continued. "I didn't say anything about it either because I knew it couldn't work. I'm no fit kind of man for you, Jenny."

"No, no." Jenny wiped her eyes with the back of her hand. "You're a good man. I was wrong to judge you the way I did in the beginning."

Beck looked at the ground.

"We can take Dave and go far away. We can be a family together. Safe. You and I could ... could be married."

John searched the sky in his struggle to find words. "Our worlds. Our worlds are too different. The way I've lived and what I thought for so long is all slipping away. The West that I always knew is disappearing. When it is gone, me and my kind will go with it. A man in my business is lucky if he sees thirty. I'm thirty-six, Jenny, I'm just too old. I'm too old for us."

Jenny shook her head in protest.

"The crazy thing is that a man can waste years of his life for nothing.

Then, when he finds what's truly worthwhile, it's too late. But, I'll tell you one thing for sure. No matter what happens tomorrow, I wouldn't trade one minute of this year I've spent with you and Dave for anything. Not one minute."

Jenny looked down for a moment and then spoke with attempted lightness. "Look at me, I'm shaking. It must be getting cold."

"Yeah. I reckon you ought to be going back to the cabin now."

Jenny started to turn down the path, but Beck stopped her. "Jenny. There's one other thing. What you said about Jesus being willing to die for others. I understand that now. Will you say a prayer for me tomorrow?"

At that moment, Jenny ran into Beck's arms, and they held each other as if never to let go. She pressed her cheek against his chest.

They held each other for a long time, Jenny looking small and delicate but safe, wrapped in John Beck's powerful arms. Finally, he gently pushed her away by the shoulders and smoothed back a strand of dark hair from her face. She looked up into his eyes and whispered, "Don't make me go yet. Let me stay a little longer." He took her hand and led her to the rim of the hill where they sat back against a log and watched the last of the sun's fire settle into embers.

After the moon arose to light the mountain with silver radiance, I still struggled within myself. I wanted so much to be included within the circumference of their feelings. Yet, I knew it would be wrong to interrupt their last moment together. I had persuaded myself to slip back to the cabin when Beck turned and whispered something to Jenny. She didn't respond, having fallen asleep nestled against his shoulder. I was afraid to move then and waited as Beck lifted Jenny in his arms and carried her like a sleeping child back to the cabin.

I waited a minute, then followed.

As I stepped through the door of our cabin, Beck stood in the main room, starting the process of inspecting, cleaning, and reloading all of the available weapons. "You can stay with me for a while if you want, Dave." At that moment, welling up with unspoken love and loyalty for the man, I determined to stay awake with him for the whole night. I would ride with him anywhere to face our enemies in combat. But, even as I sat, forming these plans, I too fell asleep.

Chapter 28

THE MORNING SUN shone through the windows. John Beck was gone. So began the waiting, the clock ticking through the hours. Preparing and nibbling breakfast that nobody wanted. Little conversation and more than a little pacing about. Once, Jenny broke the silence by remarking, "He's probably in town by now."

At about noon I got up from my chair and stepped toward the door, "I'm going out and get the horses ready to leave, just in case." When Jenny looked like she might protest, I added, "It's the way John wanted it."

Minutes later, Jenny and I gathered food and a few things to take with us. Jenny glanced out the window and hurried to the door. "John's back!"

I gave a quick look out the window at the lone rider on the ridge as I followed her. I stopped in my tracks when she halted in the open doorway. "God help us." She gasped.

Rushing to Jenny's side, my stomach turned with a sick wave of horror as I recognized the approaching rider. It was Jud Sykes. Behind him rode a dozen or more horsemen.

I bolted the door and opened the windows, practicing aiming my rifle through them. Jenny placed boxes of ammunition within easy reach. Everything apparently ready, we crouched behind the cabin wall, watched through a window, and waited. Neither of us said anything about what John Beck's absence meant. But that bitter awareness left a terrible resolve in me to wreak as much punishment as possible against the men who lined the far bank of the creek.

Sykes separated from the group and came forward, carrying a white flag on a stick.

I belted on Pa's .44 and stepped to the door, then motioned for Jenny to come close. "Stand just behind the doorpost," I instructed as she cocked the rifle she held. "Just hold the Winchester straight out where I can reach for it, quick, with little movement. I stood in the doorway leaning against the right doorframe. My heart pounded like a threshing machine.

Jud stopped before the porch and dropped the truce flag. He grinned with his usual sneer. "Time's come to leave, squatter." He spoke as if he had already won. "Mr. Maxwell asked me to come an' tell you real nice one more time."

"And if we don't?"

Jud's grin broadened. "Well, now, Mr. Maxwell will git the ranch anyway. You git to keep a part of it— about six feet down." He paused for a second, savoring his next comment, "And don't you worry. I'll take good care of your sister."

Jud tensed, ready to draw, apparently assuming I would go into a rage of hasty action. With every fiber of my being, I ached to draw my weapon and shoot away that taunting grin. Yet, I remained steady.

Jud relaxed a little. He seemed disappointed. "All right, boy. This is your last chance. Maxwell told me to let you go if you'd just ride out."

"So you can follow us later and shoot us in the back, like you did our pa?"

Jud stiffened again.

Suddenly, a wave of compassion washed over me. "Jud, ride away from here now. Far away. Pray and repent. Get married and raise a family. Live a good life. There's still time."

Sykes leaned back with a disbelieving look. He paused in thought. I waited.

The man shook his head and laughed. "Boy, you shore are crazy. I knew the first time I laid eyes on you, I was gonna have to kill you."

A kind of peace wrapped in sadness came to me as I accepted the inevitable. "I know you have to try. Look at the ground around you."

Sykes' face contorted in hate. He went for his gun.

I ducked behind the doorframe as a bullet buzzed by my ear, ripping away a splinter of wood. Grabbing the rifle from Jenny, I lunged back into the open and fired. The weapon bucked against my shoulder. Jud fell backward as his horse bolted away.

Taking no chances, I levered another shell into the rifle and fired into the jerking body on the ground. It went still. When the smoke cleared, the man who had been Jud Sykes was no more.

My stomach sickened as I realized the significance of what I had just done. "Oh, God. Dear God, forgive me."

"Dave! Get back in the house."

I barely noticed Jenny screaming but came to my senses at the roar of gunfire and bullets hitting the door next to me. I ducked back inside.

"They're coming," Jenny shouted.

Standing with my back pressed against the wall, I saw Jenny aim her rifle out the window. No time for moralizing now, I pointed my weapon through the window next to my sister. All the remaining riders galloped their horses, hell-bent, straight at us, firing as they came. The ground rumbled with hoof beats.

We fired back, but there were too many of them, rushing us too fast. In moments, the outlaws would overwhelm our meager fortress and come flooding onto the porch and through the door to take our lives.

They peppered our cabin with bullets. Jenny winced as one splintered the windowsill. The coffeepot flew off the stove and clattered against the stovepipe.

We ducked behind the wall. Jenny looked over at me, her eyes wide.

"Jenny, the dynamite. Wait for my signal."

I ventured a peek around the edge of the window. The lead riders were almost between the hidden boxes. Paying no attention to the bullet that removed my hat, I aimed and followed Beck's instructions. *Distance and elevation. Squeeze the trigger.*

The world seemed to explode before me with a deafening roar. Horses and men screamed and fell away from the belch of flame and smoke. All was pandemonium as other riders tried to control their bucking mounts. Most turned to run back to cover when Jenny's second shot detonated the other box of dynamite.

When the smoke cleared, one horse and rider were down. One man limped away while the rest crouched behind the protection of the creek bank. They fired sporadically with little effect. "That should keep them down for a while," I said.

"Yes, but how long?" Jenny continued to reload her rifle.

I couldn't answer. A new fear plagued me. Our assailants would be cautious now, thinking up a new strategy. What would that be?

#

Occasional shots kept us alert for another half hour. Without warning, a barrage of shots pelted the log walls like a heavy rain. Risking a glance from the lower corner of the window, I noticed a man in a Mexican-style sombrero break away from his companions and slip into the forest.

"They're trying to get somebody behind us. Stay here, Jenny, and take a shot once in a while to make them think they still have our attention. I'll check the back."

"Be careful."

From the window in Pa's room, I could see the outlaw clambering down the hill behind our cabin. I could not get a good shot as he ducked from tree to tree. I needed something that would cover some space without taking time to aim. Stepping into the front room, I grabbed Pa's shotgun from its pegs above the mantel.

When I looked through the bedroom window again, the man was nowhere to be seen. The best hiding spot was behind the outhouse. On that assumption, I pointed the long barrels of the shotgun at the lower right corner of the little building.

The recoil of the twelve gauge nearly knocked me off my feet. Its roar was overwhelmed by the blast of the dynamite. Boards, splinters and other debris filled the air. When it cleared away, the hatless outlaw, his clothes tattered and blackened, ran up the steep slope with the fleetness of a squirrel scurrying up a tree. He must have decided to move on to safer parts because he never returned to the fight.

#

Nothing moved for a while. No shots. Everyone waited. The possibilities grated on my mind. When night came on, our enemies would make another move. With us tiring and less alert, they would try to sneak in. They could try to set the cabin on fire. Would that be our end?

"Jenny, I'm sorry I didn't get us out of here sooner."

"It's all right. God will see us through this, somehow. I hope." She grew quiet for a couple minutes, watching out the window. "It will be good to be with Momma and Papa."

My heart sank. "Yes, it will." I changed the subject. "I just wish I knew what Maxwell's men would try next."

Jenny held up a box. "We are running low on ammunition."

"I know."

"I never imagined we would use so much."

We both fell silent for several minutes.

"Dave?"

"Yeah?" I continued watching the creek bank.

"Dave?"

I turned and looked into my sister's moist eyes.

"I know I never said it much, but … I've always loved you. You're the best brother anyone could ask for."

"I love you too, Sis." I could hardly get my words around the lump in my throat because I knew we were saying goodbye.

#

A rider appeared on the ridge. He spurred his horse to a cluster of aspen trees about halfway down and to the left side of the slope. From his tall, white Stetson hat and black frock coat, I could tell it was Frank Maxwell.

He waited as a man, his regular foreman I assumed, rode up to him. Their conversation appeared animated and angry. Maxwell pointed toward the men at the river, and the foreman rode back.

"Jenny, that's Maxwell."

"I thought so."

"You know, we might be able to end this fight right now." I raised my rifle.

"It's a long shot."

"Yeah, but it's worth a bullet to try." I aimed my gun sights on the man then raised them to compensate for the distance.

Just at that moment, a vision came to me as clear the day I remembered sitting on a log at the creek. The look in Frank Maxwell's eyes as he remembered his boy and his wife. The pain I saw there. The man who had been a different man than the villain I knew. Someone who had been human with a family.

I hesitated.

"Shoot before he moves." Jenny looked tense in my peripheral vision.

I hesitated. I could feel the sweat dampening my forehead.

"Dave, shoot."

The front sight wavered on such a small target. I held my breath then let it out slowly to keep the rifle barrel steady—and pulled the trigger. I felt it, the slight jerk of my hand.

The weapon bucked and smoked, sending out its deadly missile. A breath of breeze pushed the smoke past my vision, but the target still sat steady upon his saddle. I waited. Then I saw it, a puff of dust a foot ahead of his horse's feet. The animal shied sideways, and Maxwell looked toward us. He moved with his mount back farther into the concealment of the trees.

Disappointed, I turned to see Jenny leave the room then return with a bed sheet. Drawing a knife from a drawer, she cut a strip. "What are you doing, Sis?"

She looked me straight in the eye. "Bandages."

I moved over and opened the door, then took a position behind it. She paused in her work. "Now what are you doing?"

"If I shoot from here, it will draw some of the fire away from you."

Jenny said nothing but piled strips of material on the table.

Through the door I could see the tops of men's hats moving about, gathering around the foreman. He soon rode back up toward his boss. They were ready to make a move. My grip tightened on the rifle.

I looked up at something that caught my attention from the top of the ridge. A lone rider. A big man on a big buckskin horse. My heart leaped.

John Beck!

Chapter 29

JOHN BECK NOW sat on his horse upon the ridge. He remained still as if scrutinizing the scene below.

"Maxwell's men haven't noticed him yet," I said as I hurried to reload my rifle. Indeed, none of the outlaws had seen the new warrior in the battle. The small clump of aspens also hid Beck from Maxwell and his foreman.

"How will John ever get to us?" Jenny said.

"I don't know, sneak around to the back maybe."

Beck drew his rifle like a sword from its saddle scabbard. Then, resting the butt against his hip, so the weapon tilted upward, he walked his horse down the slope. Magnificent and courageous, like a knight of old, riding into battle. Fear welled up in me when I realized what he planned to do.

"Oh no!" Jenny gasped. "He's going to charge them head on. He won't have a chance. "We've got to give him all the cover we can." We raised our rifles.

Beck's horse increased speed to a trot. The rider came steadily on with grim resolve. In a moment, he would reach the place where the slope leveled off. Also, he would be past the aspens where he would be within Maxwell's view, thereby losing the element of surprise.

My heart pounded. I ached to stop time, change the day, but nothing on Earth could now halt the devastating clash about to come.

Before we fired a shot, our enemies made their move. Three men ran from cover across the clearing at us. Firing as they came, they ran in a zigzag fashion, making them hard to hit. Another one disappeared into the trees to the right while the rest continued to shoot at us from the cover of the bank.

Jenny and I returned the fire. I shot a third time at the man running in the lead and saw him go down. Another went down as he reached the porch before Jenny's window. The third man ducked onto the porch behind the wall.

"I'm out of bullets," Jenny yelled.

I tossed the shotgun to her.

A wild rebel yell echoed across the valley, and John Beck exploded into action. The horse lunged into full gallop. Startled gunmen turned to see him descending upon them, as swift and terrible as an eagle swooping upon its prey.

Dropping the reins, he guided his steed with his legs. Firing as rapidly as the Winchester's lever would allow, he sent a deadly rain of bullets among the outlaws. All turning upon their assailant, men shot and cursed and fell. Beck raced on, the fringes of his jacket fluttering in the wind. At the same time, I hit an outlaw who had stood to take aim at Beck. I fired shot after shot to cover our friend. Another man staggered and dropped behind the bank. Two ran away into the forest.

Beck's hat flew off. He jerked and wavered in the saddle as another bullet struck him. I winced as if I had been hit myself. But he kept coming. I wanted to cry and cheer at the same time. He was at once magnificent and yet pitiful as he charged on, carelessly pouring out his life for us into the fire of our enemies.

Two men mounted their horses. Beck shot one from the saddle. The second man struggled to control his panic-stricken horse, so Beck was almost on him before the outlaw brought up his pistol. Beck attempted a shot at him, but the rifle must have been empty. He threw the gun, knocking the man off balance. With no time left to yank the thong from the holster and draw his own pistol, Beck tore the Bowie knife from its sheath, and, wielding it like a sword, slashed the second rider from his mount.

Without breaking stride, Beck drove on, splashing through the creek, explosions of water spraying from the horse's pounding hooves. With his huge, gleaming knife held out like a saber, Beck continued to roar defiance like an enraged grizzly.

A puff of gun smoke rose up from behind the bank where the last gunman crouched, concealed from my sights. When Beck hit dry ground, he reined up hard and threw the knife. As it descended, another shot roared from behind the bank. Beck fell backward from his horse.

Then, silence. Nothing moved except a riderless horse wandering away from that desolate scene.

Jenny screamed. "Behind you!"

Spinning around, I dropped to a knee. A man stood in the bedroom doorway, aiming a pistol at me. My rifle clicked on an empty chamber.

Thunder boomed, and the gunman flew backward through the bedroom doorway. To my right, Jenny leaned against the wall, wide-eyed, with the smoking shotgun in her hands.

I smiled and nodded to her. In that moment, a shot roared over my shoulder, and my sister fell.

Drawing Pa's .44, I spun and shot the man standing in the front doorway. He staggered back, firing in reaction. Pain seared across my thigh. I fired again. The outlaw tumbled back, disappearing below the edge of the porch.

I ran to my sister. "Jenny!" Kneeling, I raised her to a sitting position. She shook her head as if clearing a daze.

"I ... I think I'm all right, just grazed, I think. A streak of red stained the side of her blouse.

I grabbed a long bandage from the table. "Here, let me help you."

She snatched the cloth from me. "No, no, go help John."

As I hurried back to the door, Jenny started bandaging her own wound. I was never so proud of her.

The valley was strewn with death, except for two riders coming down the slope. Beck was hidden by the near edge of the creek bank. Alive or dead, I knew not.

And then John Beck rose and stood on wavering legs. He dragged his pistol from its holster and fired a single shot at the other gunman behind the bank.

Shots rang out behind Beck. The two men on the slope galloped toward him. The one in the lead was Maxwell's foreman.

Beck, his left arm dangling at his side, staggered back into the creek, trying to reach the cover of the other bank. Too late. In the middle of the creek, bullets sent up little spouts of water dangerously close. Steadying himself, Beck aimed and fired at the approaching rider. The gunman jerked sideways in the saddle but hung on to the saddle horn. He kept coming. Beck's second shot took him as he entered the creek. The man toppled into the water with a great splash just a few feet from where Beck stood.

With what appeared to be great effort, Beck struggled on across the creek to face Frank Maxwell. But Maxwell halted his mount, taking aim with his rifle. Smoke and fire belched from the barrel, and Beck fell, spinning, to the ground.

My heart stopped.

"No—*no!*" Jenny screamed as she rushed from the doorway. I shoved her back inside and ran. Beck crawled to reach the pistol that had fallen from his hand while Maxwell walked his horse ever closer to finish his grim work.

I ran full out, trying to get into pistol range, firing a vain shot to distract Maxwell's attention. It worked. He turned and fired at me. I dropped down to the edge of the creek as his bullet hit the bank behind me.

At the creek, I was in range. I fired with more care as he levered another bullet. To my surprise, the rifle jerked from Maxwell's hands. I was disappointed, though. I had been aiming at his heart.

My enemy drew his pistol, thus beginning a deadly game of wills. Without thought of fear or death, I concentrated on the sights of the heavy pistol in my hand and marched on through the creek. Step forward, aim, and fire. Step forward, aim ... Pay no notice to Maxwell firing, or sand and water kicking up around me. *Squeeze the trigger.*

From the corner of my eye, I saw John Beck struggle up on his elbow and slowly raise his pistol toward our opponent. Maxwell caught the movement, turned, and aimed at the man on the ground.

This was my last shot. As much as every fiber of my being cried out for it, I could not fire in haste. *Aim—slow breath—squeeze.*

Three shots rang out together. I watched, breathless, through the clearing smoke. The universe seemed to pause to await the verdict of this moment.

Maxwell sat straight in his saddle, then leaned over as if looking with curiosity at Beck. Leaning still farther, he fell from his horse.

Beck lowered his weapon and his body to the earth. He lay still. The war was over.

#

I don't know how long I stood in a daze, looking at the destruction around me. I came to myself as I noticed the damp coldness of the creek chilling my legs. A deep weariness weighed upon me. I looked over at the place where Beck lay, limp and motionless—could not approach his body yet—my mind not ready to accept what I knew I would find.

My next thought was to take care of my sister. Limping back to the cabin, I first realized the pain in my upper leg where a bullet had grazed it. My cheek stung also, reminding me how close death had come. I found Jenny leaning against the inside wall. Hands over her ears, eyes closed, her lips moving in silent prayer.

"Jenny."

She stared at me, the fearful, unspoken question in her eyes. I couldn't speak. I just shook my head.

Jenny began to cry, and I took her into my arms. We wept together without shame. Not only for John but for all that had been lost that day. The wasted lives sacrificed to the root of all evil. The personal death within us—the death of our innocence.

Jenny pushed back from our embrace. Her voice was low as she said, "We need to see to him, now." She took my hand, and we limped across the clearing. It was a long walk, the longest we would ever take together.

Someone once said that the saddest thing next to losing a war is winning a war. I understood as we passed the silent bodies on that bloody field. I understood the sadness in my father's eyes when he remembered back. A sadness that would be a part of me now.

Jenny knelt beside Beck and stroked his cheek. "Oh, John." She put her hand on his shoulder.

I turned away to allow her this private moment when she jerked her hand away. "He moved. He's alive!"

"Jenny, no, that's impossible ..." Hoof beats sounded behind me. Spinning around, I instinctively reached for my gun.

"Whoa, there. I just came to help." It was Luke Dawson. Joe Warner sat on another horse behind him. The two men stepped down from their mounts and took off their hats."

Joe Warner's voice sounded low and husky as he spoke. "Sure am sorry about the trouble you folks had. I'll have to tell y' though, Beck sure put up a bully fight in town. Faced Fallon head on, he did. Fallon was fast, but Beck was as fast. When the smoke cleared Fallon went down for good."

"Beck's an honorable man. Waited for Fallon to draw first. Then he drew like greased lightning," Luke Dawson added.

Warner smiled. "Ol' Luke here shot one of Maxwell's men that tried to back shoot Beck from the loft window of the livery."

Dawson shook his head. "Can't abide no ambushers."

We all watched as Jenny raised Beck's head upon her lap. He opened his eyes and looked up at her, his voice weak. "Jenny? You shouldn't … be out here. It … ain't safe."

Tears rolled down Jenny's cheeks, but she smiled bravely. "No, John, no. It's all right. It's over. We're safe now."

Managing a small smile and nod, John Beck closed his eyes. He looked … peaceful.

Chapter 30

I AROSE JUST before dawn. It was habit now. I lit the lantern, stoked the fireplace, and started water heating for coffee. Jenny would be up before long to prepare breakfast. I strapped on my old .44, also a habit now, and went out to the new barn to feed the stock.

A hard September rain had blown through the valley the previous night. I had to step around puddles. Sunlight broke over the mountain ridges, lighting the first autumn gold on the aspens. A light glowed in the barn, which I didn't expect.

I stepped inside and spoke to the back of the man who was just taking a bridle from its wall peg. "You know, a couple times in my life I've seen what I would call miracles. You surviving that shootout was one of them."

"It sure came as a surprise to me, too." John Beck led his horse from its stall. The man walked with a pronounced limp. "What with Joe Warner digging four bullets out of me."

"It was the one close to your heart that had us worried the most."

He smiled, giving the tip of his mustache a little twist. "Well, I guess I couldn't die the way your sister hovered over me like a mother hen all those weeks."

"She was a regular drill sergeant."

With a groan, Beck heaved his saddle up on his horse. "That was a good decision to hire Luke Dawson to help around here. He's a good hand. Reliable—works hard."

"I'll be able to pay him better in the spring when the mares drop their foals, and we're back in the horse business again." I noticed through the window that a light flickered to life in the new bunkhouse. Luke was probably up, getting ready for daily chores. "I think he stays on here mostly to be around Jenny."

Beck chuckled. "Not too hard to figure that one out."

"Yep."

Beck led his horse out of the barn. I followed.

"John, are you going hunting or something?"

"No."

"Town?"

"No."

"Then where?"

He looked down as he stroked his mustache. "Well, I'm moving on." His voice grew husky. "Time to be moving on."

"But why?" A fear gripped my chest. I had suspected this might happen, but I didn't want to admit it to myself.

He didn't look at me as he tightened the cinch on the saddle. "My job's done here. I told you a long time ago I'd just stay until you all could take care of yourselves. You can do that now. He looked over at the cabin. "Besides, I got business that's been waiting for me."

"Where will you go?"

"Oh, Arizona, maybe." He rolled and rubbed a stiff shoulder, the area of another wound. "The cold of the high country gets to my bones nowadays."

Beck checked the contents of his saddlebags. He reached in and pulled out a sack of jerky and other edibles. Meeting his approval, he put it back in. Then came two boxes of .45 shells. One was empty, so he threw it away. Next, to his apparent surprise, he pulled out Jenny's Bible. "You folks should keep this. It's got your family names and such in it."

I guess, somehow, Jenny must have sensed that John would leave before I did. Or maybe she was just more honest with herself. "She wants you to have it."

He smiled and shook his head. "That sister of yours never gives up. Well …" He sighed, "Who knows? She might just get me converted yet." He put the Bible back into the saddlebag.

The smile left his face then as he turned and looked at the cabin for a long time. He stared toward the place where Jenny still slept, a shadow of sadness in his eyes. "Yeah, it's time to move on. That's just the way it is."

Riding away had to be the hardest thing John Beck would ever do. Harder than facing blizzards or grizzlies or armed men.

"Please don't go, John. You don't have to go now. We all want you to stay. She wants you to stay."

"Yeah, I know." His voice was low as he looked back at the cabin. "But the time is right." He kicked away a small stone on the barn floor. "That Luke Dawson is a good man, a real good man. He'll have his own place someday. Make a woman a fine husband, good provider, good father for his kids."

I nodded and looked at the ground. "Wherever you go, our prayers will go with you."

He smiled. "I'll appreciate that."

"Will you be coming back?"

"Sure, I'll be back around sometime. Maybe you and me will go hunting and fishing."

"Yeah ... Yeah, that would be good."

He finally looked at me and said, "I ain't one for making speeches, but I'm glad to have spent this time with you." He smiled. "I'll always be proud to say I rode with Dave Foster. And, well ..."

Things got kind of uncomfortable then. "Here." He handed me Pa's pocketknife. I held the gift, trying to hold back the vice of pain squeezing my heart. I couldn't look up as I said, "This was a gift for you."

"I know, but ... a young fella ought to have his pa's things."

"Thanks for all you did for us."

"And thank you."

I looked up. "For what?"

"More than you know, son."

I wanted to hug John Beck. But in those days, I thought it was unmanly. I reached out my hand. "Well ... goodbye, sir."

Beck took my hand. "I know you'll take care of your sister and the ranch and all."

I nodded.

John hugged me. It was quick, strong, and kind of awkward. "You're a good boy."

Then he held me out with his big hands on my shoulders. "No ... no." He shook his head then looked me straight in the eyes. "You're a good *man*."

Beck turned to mount up but paused, leaning a moment against his saddle as if facing a great effort. He forced his stiff leg to bend to the stirrup, and with a groan, heaved himself up onto the horse.

I watched John Beck ride away. Watched as he spurred his horse up the slope to the top of the ridge.

Once there, he stopped to look once more over our valley. Just like the first day I saw him sitting up there, big and rugged and alone. He turned his horse and disappeared into the shimmering gold of the aspens.

The air was clear and fresh from the previous night's rain and with it, the feel of autumn. The last clouds drifted away beyond the mountains. The storm had left our valley.

Epilogue

The Good Book says that there is a season for all things. Those seasons move on. Jenny married Luke Dawson. They and their family have a thriving ranch of their own in Montana.

I still raise good horses. Sarah and I and our son James John Foster live about a mile upstream from the old homeplace. Too many ghosts of memories keep us away from that forlorn spot.

I heard occasional rumors about John Beck in the years after he left. One claimed that he moved up to Denver and became a Pinkerton detective. Another was that he married a widow, a lady preacher, up in Wyoming. Beyond such questionable pieces of information, facts of Beck's future were even more mysterious than those of his past.

The closest I came to finding him occurred fifteen years after he left us, and I was on my own, writing for a newspaper after serving a short time as a lawman. Following a slim lead, I found a small wooden marker in a cemetery outside Globe, Arizona, a little town nestled in the Tonto Rim country. The marker's inscription read only, J. BECK. I asked around, but nobody seemed to remember him until I went to the town marshal.

"Yeah, I seem to recall there was a fella named Beck that served as a deputy for the marshal before me. Don't remember his first name." The lawman scratched at one of his sideburns. "He married the widow Abernathy. Yep, Hannah Abernathy. That was her name."

"Was she a lady preacher by any chance?"

He chuckled. "No, but I heard that they were good, church-goin' folks."

"How did he die?"

"Now, that was kinda ironic. Some old timers say he was out on patrol one night. A drunk in an alley shot him in the back, thinking it was the marshal. Never knew what hit him. His wife passed on in her sleep less than a year later."

I thanked the marshal and, on an impulse, went to the local stone cutter. From him I bought two new, respectable tombstones to replace the old, faded markers. On one I repeated original words:

Hannah Beck,
Beloved wife

On the other I put:

J. Beck
Beloved husband *and father*

Those who did not know him as I did would not understand the meaning of the inscription.

I do not know for sure if it was the John Beck that I knew in that grave. Putting the finishing words on the tombstone gave me a sense of completeness, though. Yet, there is a part of me that wants to believe he is still out there somewhere.

#

The world has changed since I was thirteen. There are telephones, horseless carriages, and even talk of machines that can fly. The West has lost much of its wildness and natural boldness. Yet, whenever I look at my father's old pocketknife where it sits on my desk, I am taken back to those days of untamed wilderness, grizzly bears, and wild horse herds roaming free. Once again, I see John Beck up on the ridge above our valley, silent and threatening like a thunderhead on the horizon.

He taught me much about life and death and growing up. I learned courage, honor, and respect for women. I learned about not judging others until you stand awhile in their boots. He taught me how to be a man.

He was wrong about one thing, though. He once said that when the West, the Old West, was gone, he would go with it. It was the other way around. When he was gone, the West went with him.